**"I'll be yo~~ur~~**
**running his ~~hand along the~~**
**neck and pacing some more.**

Caitlyn stared at him. "No."

"It's that or protective custody. Your choice, Caitlyn."

A world-weary sigh hissed out of her.

Pressure welled up in his chest. Why did she always have to fight him? He didn't want to scare her any more than he already had. But she left him no choice.

"Don't argue with me, Caitlyn. This guy could be waiting at your house."

Her bottomless eyes grew huge. Speechless for four, five, six full seconds. The longest he'd ever known Caitlyn to stay silent.

"Just work with me here." Mitch sat back down.

Something in her eyes softened.

Had she heard the desperation in his plea?

Seeing her again had stirred up every memory and feeling he thought he'd buried. He might be desperate to keep her safe, but he was just as desperate to win her love again.

**Books by Shannon Taylor Vannatter**

Love Inspired Heartsong Presents

*Rodeo Regrets*
*Rodeo Queen*

## SHANNON TAYLOR VANNATTER

is a stay-at-home mom and pastor's wife. Her debut novel won a 2011 Inspirational Readers' Choice Award. When not writing, she runs circles in the care and feeding of her husband, their son and their church congregation. Home is a central Arkansas zoo with two charcoal-gray cats, a chocolate Lab and three dachshunds in weenie-dog heaven. If given the chance to clean house or write, she'd rather write. Her goal is to hire Alice from the Brady Bunch.

# SHANNON TAYLOR VANNATTER

# Rodeo Queen

HEARTSONG
PRESENTS

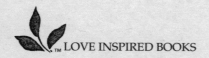 LOVE INSPIRED BOOKS

Recycling programs for this product may not exist in your area.

ISBN-13: 978-0-373-48682-3

RODEO QUEEN

Copyright © 2013 by Shannon Taylor Vannatter

www.Harlequin.com

**Printed in U.S.A.**

But let all those that put their trust in thee rejoice: let them ever shout for joy, because thou defendest them: let them also that love thy name be joyful in thee.
—*Psalms* 5:11

I dedicate this book to my son, Logan,
for putting up with Mom glued to the computer
and for bragging that his mom's a writer.

# Chapter 1

Was he waiting for her?

A chill crept up Caitlyn Wentworth's spine—a chill that had nothing to do with mid-September in Texas. Was he out there tonight? In the rodeo arena?

She smoothed shaky hands over her sequined sapphire top and rhinestone-studded white jeans. The matching glitter on her cowgirl hat flashed as she adjusted it and checked her reflection in the dressing-room mirror. Shaky or not, the show had to go on.

"What's this?" Natalie's tone was a bit shrill.

The letter Caitlyn had gotten today dangled from her sister's hand.

"Nothing." Caitlyn snatched it.

"Nothing?" Natalie snatched the letter back and read it aloud. "'Who do you think you are leaving me and our boy? Did you really think you could get away? I know exactly where you are. Camille.'"

Caitlyn grabbed at the letter, but Natalie turned away

and kept reading. "'And when you're least expecting it, I'll be there. I'll grab that long dark hair and drag you back home where you belong.'" Natalie's hand shook. "Where did you get this? Who is Camille?"

"It came in the mail, and I don't know who Camille is, but he seems to think I'm her."

"Who's he?"

Why hadn't she played dumb and pretended the letter was in her locker by mistake?

"Some guy who apparently thinks I'm Camille." Caitlyn nabbed the letter, stuffed it on the top shelf with the others and clicked the padlock in place.

"Is this the only letter?"

*Yes* hovered on the tip of Caitlyn's tongue. But she was a terrible liar. Her gaze darted from her sister's. "No."

"How many?" Natalie shot Caitlyn her best you'd-better-tell-me-everything glare.

"Six." Caitlyn sighed.

"Six?" Natalie's blue eyes widened. "Have you called the police?"

No police. Calling police would spin her carefully ordered, Mitchless life out of control. Caitlyn rolled her eyes, trying to hide her panic. "He hasn't done anything but send me letters."

"Are they all threatening like this one?"

It wasn't her imagination. The letter *was* threatening. The first one that made her heart quiver. "No. Just kind of whiny and poor me."

"Why haven't you called the police?"

"Because I figure he's a harmless, confused coward. Obviously, I'm not Camille."

"Well, he thinks you are and wants to drag *you* home by *your* hair." Natalie propped her hands on her hips. "I'm not sure why you think he's a coward. We need to call the police."

"No." Caitlyn tried to sound calm. "Letter writers are like Peeping Toms. They don't do anything but write letters."

"Who says? Dr. Phil?"

"I don't have time to watch Dr. Phil. It's nothing, Nat. Just forget it."

"It's not nothing. I'm calling Mitch." Natalie fished her cell from her purse.

Caitlyn's heart lurched and she lunged toward Natalie. "No."

"He'll know what to do."

A knot lodged in her throat. "You don't even know his number."

"He's in my address book."

Her breath stalled. "Why?"

"Back when I was in my bar-hopping mode—" Natalie sighed "—I ran into him. He was on duty, but he saw me and offered to drive me back to my apartment. I refused, but he still made me see the error of my ways and asked about you."

Caitlyn's brain whirled. Mitch had tried to rescue Natalie from herself. And asked about Caitlyn. "I'm glad he tried to help you."

"Actually, I think he did help me." Natalie shrugged. "But back to the problem at hand. Give me one good reason I shouldn't make the call."

"Because I don't think it's a big deal, but if I get another letter like that, I'll call the police." Caitlyn closed her eyes. "Just not him."

"And you'll tell me if you get another?" Natalie's gaze narrowed. "Of any kind?"

"Yes."

"Promise?"

"Yes." And she never broke a promise. *Please, Lord, don't let there be another.*

"All right." Natalie slid the phone back in her purse.

"What are you doing nosing around in my locker anyway?"

"Getting your jewelry bag like you asked me to." Natalie held up the clear, plastic bag. Rhinestones flickered in the light.

"Thanks." Caitlyn unzipped the bag and fastened the shimmering necklace in place, then slid the matching studs in her ears.

How could she forget the letter was there? It had rattled her from the moment she'd arrived at Cowtown Coliseum this evening and Glen had given her a stack of mail. Most of her fan letters were from little girls who wanted to be rodeo queens just like her when they grew up. A few came from brazen cowboys asking for a date with their phone numbers included.

Until these letters to Camille.

Six letters in as many weeks.

"See you later." Caitlyn slipped into her red-white-and-blue-sequined jacket, then strode through the back lobby to the corral. Her white horse, Lightning, waited, saddled and ready.

An aging rodeo hand held the American flag for her as she mounted her steed. "Evening, Caitlyn."

"Hi, Pete. Looks like a big crowd tonight."

He handed her the flag as her cue began—the opening notes of "God Bless the U.S.A." Caitlyn nudged her horse into the arena. The spotlight blinded her.

Was he out there watching? Waiting in the darkened crowd to drag her out by her hair? Goose bumps crawled over her skin.

No time to worry about it now. She snapped her reins and Lightning made the first round, the flag waving proudly behind them. As the song sped up, she urged her horse to pick up her pace until the song built to its climax and she was charging her horse around the arena.

As queen at the Fort Worth Stockyards Championship Rodeo, every Friday and Saturday night she made runs around the arena carrying flags representing individual sponsors. But the initial opening run with the American flag was her favorite. Though she'd heard the song countless times, she never tired of it. At the end of the ride, she never failed to feel more American.

The last notes faded away and she darted out of the arena on Lightning. The crowd roared behind her. She shivered at the thought that her letter writer might be roaring, as well.

Mitch had connections in every law enforcement agency in the state. If she went to the police, he'd find out and he'd come to her rescue. Her heart couldn't take another run-in with Mitch Warren.

No. She'd have to handle the letters on her own.

"Great job as usual, Caitlyn." Pete met her near the corral and took her final flag for the evening. Only the second round of bulls was left, but her flag-bearing duties were done until tomorrow night.

"Thanks." All she needed to do was change clothes and go home. But the dark outside waited. What if the letter writer wasn't a coward? Did he know what she drove? Was he waiting in her car?

Natalie had rattled her. But it wouldn't hurt to have backup. "Do you think you could walk me out tonight, Pete?"

"I'll see you out." Glen, her boss's assistant appeared out of nowhere. "Bob wants to see you in the office before you leave, though."

"Now?"

"It seemed urgent."

She frowned. "What for?"

"Didn't say." Glen shrugged skinny shoulders. "Just let me know when you're ready."

Why would her boss want to see her? Trying to ooze confidence, she strode through the lobby to the office and knocked on the door.

"Come in." Bob's gruff voice came through the thick wood.

Caitlyn swung the door open.

Ornate wood-paneled walls framed Bob sitting at his desk, frowning. "Sit down."

"Is something wrong?"

"You tell me. Your sister told me about the letters."

*Natalie.* Caitlyn's jaw dropped. How could she?

"Don't you think you should have told someone about this? Me? The police?"

"This is the first one that's…" Caitlyn sank to the bench lining the office wall.

"Threatening."

"Natalie shouldn't have bothered you with this."

"Your sister is worried about you and, quite frankly, so am I." The seriousness in Bob's voice tugged at her, making the letters seem even more worrisome.

Despite shaking legs, Caitlyn stood. "What do you plan to—"

A knock sounded at the door. She jumped.

"Come in." Bob sounded even gruffer. "That's probably Ranger Warren. He'll be handling the case for us."

Warren? Her dazed brain stopped functioning.

The door opened and Mitch Warren strode in. His cowboy hat shadowed short dark hair and vivid sea-green eyes capable of looking into her soul.

Ten years since high school. He'd gotten even better looking.

"Hello, Caitlyn." His rich, honeyed baritone turned her name into a caress.

Weak-kneed, she sank to the bench again.

"Aren't you going to say hello?" He tipped his hat in her direction.

"You two know each other?"

"We went to school together."

*We were high school sweethearts.* Her heart still hadn't recovered. *Say something. Stop staring like a slack-jawed teenager.* She licked her lips and forced her gaze away from him back to Bob. "You called the Texas Rangers?"

"I'm trying to look out for the safety of my staff."

She covered her face with both hands. "This isn't necessary."

"From the sound of that letter, I think it is." Mitch walked toward her. "I need to see all of them."

Too close. She caught a whiff of spicy, woodsy cologne. Thank goodness she was already sitting down. "They're in my locker."

"When did they start coming?"

"My second weekend as queen. About six weeks ago."

"How much time in between letters?"

A sigh escaped her. "I didn't mark my calendar when they came."

"Approximate."

"I only get my mail on Fridays and Saturdays when I'm here. I've gotten one letter every Friday, but I didn't pay any attention to when they arrived here initially."

"Do you have the envelopes?"

"With the letters."

"We'll check the postmarks and maybe we can get some latent prints. Shall we go get them?"

Unable to stand if her life depended on it, she needed a moment to digest his presence. There wasn't anything personal in her locker. She grabbed her keys from her purse.

Her hands trembled as she slid her locker key off the ring

and held it out to him. "Help yourself. Glen can show you where the dressing room is. Everything's on the top shelf."

Instead of letting her drop the key into his palm, his fingers brushed against hers as he reached for it. Electricity flared and the key slid from her hand. It landed with a metallic clang near her foot, but she was powerless to pick it up.

Mitch knelt, as if he might propose. Again. Instead, he scooped up the key, almost touching her ankle.

She shivered.

"And from the looks of you—" he studied her face "—I'd say that letter upset you more than you're letting on."

Yes. Please let him think she was weak and trembling over the letter instead of him. The letter frightened her, but Mitch scared her more.

She'd barely had time to gather her thoughts before Mitch returned and Bob left her in good hands.

And now she was alone with Mitch. He settled on the bench beside her. Although there was room for another person between them, it was too close.

"I kept them in the order I found them in. Which letter came first?" Mitch held the plastic bag containing the letters in his latex-gloved hand—just like on the cop shows.

"Back to front, exactly the way they were stacked."

Mitch read the first bagged letter slowly, then sifted to the next. With each page, his frown deepened.

"Is this your jurisdiction?" Her voice shook. "This is Fort Worth, not Garland."

"Garland and Fort Worth are in my Company B."

For now, just function, she told herself. She'd throttle her sister later.

"We'll have to print you so we can eliminate yours. Natalie only handled the latest one, right?"

"Can we just forget this? I really don't think it's a big deal."

"Lots of women have thought it was no big deal. And lots of women have ended up in body bags."

A knot lodged in her throat.

"I'm sorry, Caitlyn." He touched her elbow. "I don't mean to scare you."

Flames licked up her arm and straight to her heart.

"But I want you to realize how serious this could be."

Mitch messed with her equilibrium much more than the letter writer. Caitlyn pulled away and glanced at the clock. After 2:00 a.m.

"I know it's late and you're tired." Mitch stood and paced the office. "But I wanted to get as much detail as I could while it's fresh in your mind."

"What now?"

"I'm taking you to headquarters. We'll get your prints and put you in protective custody."

"What?" She jumped up from her seat.

"We have to keep you safe until we can get this guy off the streets."

"I run a business. I have a job. Besides, it's a letter." She sliced her hand through the air. "Cowards write letters. They have no follow-through."

"Oh, really? Ever heard of the Unabomber?"

Caitlyn rolled her eyes. She'd been in the second grade and Mitch in the fourth when he'd first decided to investigate the Unabomber. "That was an extreme case."

"All the same, we don't know what we're dealing with."

"Doesn't something actually have to happen to someone before you put them under protective custody?"

"By then, it's often too late. Stalking laws have changed. A threat is enough to take action. And that last letter is a definite threat."

"But I don't have time for protective custody."

Mitch's top lip quirked. "It's not something you generally make time for."

"No, I have a clothing store here at the stockyards—and another at the mall. And I have my duties here as rodeo queen. I can't let the rodeo down."

"Knowing you, I'm certain you've hired a great manager for each store—someone who can handle things for a few weeks. And don't they have runner-up rodeo queens or something?"

"A few weeks." Her words turned into a wail. "No!"

"Okay, probably not that long."

"My managers are great." She stalked across the office. "But the rodeo has had huge turnover in the queen department. One of the main reasons I was hired was because I promised to be here. I haven't been here quite two months. I can't take off."

"Why has there been so much turnover? Have any other queens received threats?"

"No. Nothing like that. We have to be here every Friday and Saturday night. Most single women aren't okay with that."

"Why?"

"Hello?" She shrugged. "Date nights."

He grinned. "So you've been able to be so consistent because you don't have anyone to keep your date nights open for?"

She blushed. "Dating is highly overrated. I can't let Bob down."

"I spoke with Bob earlier. He's all for protective custody."

"Really?" She frowned.

"Of course. He wants you safe."

"I should have known. He's a big teddy bear. All gruff and stern when he needs to be, but marshmallow mushy on the inside. He treats us all like his kids."

"Does he have kids?" Mitch scribbled in his notebook.

"What did you write down?" Her chest squeezed. "Bob is not a suspect."

"Everyone's a suspect until we know who the perp is. What about the other staff?"

"No." She clasped both hands over her ears. "They're not suspects. No one I know would write kooky letters."

"You never know."

"Well, I do. I won't have you digging into all my friends' and coworkers' backgrounds."

"It's my job, Caitlyn. And I'll dig until I find our letter writer and escort him to jail myself. In the meantime, you'll be in protective custody, whether you like it or not."

"I have to agree to it—right?" She folded her arms across her chest and raised her chin.

Mitch had seen that look before. The sapphire sequins on her blouse flashed in the light, matching her beautiful eyes. Stubborn eyes.

He sighed. "Technically."

"I refuse."

"Caitlyn—"

"That's it. I refuse."

"All right. Then I'll arrange to be your bodyguard." Mitch ran his hand along the back of his neck and paced some more.

"No."

"It's that or protective custody. Your choice."

"Neither."

"Not one of the choices."

A world-weary sigh hissed out of her. "Can you please take me to my car?"

"I'm driving you." Mitch wagged a finger at her. "And that's your only choice."

"I'm not going to the station tonight. I'm tired."

Pressure welled up in his chest. Why did she always have to fight him? He didn't want to scare her any more than he already had. But she left him no choice.

"The station can wait until tomorrow, but I'm driving you home. Don't argue with me, Caitlyn. This guy could be waiting at your house."

Her bottomless eyes grew huge. She was speechless for four, five, six full seconds. The longest he'd ever known Caitlyn to stay silent.

"I'll go to Mama and Daddy's. It'll freak them out if a ranger shows up."

"I'll let them know it's me."

"No. No way. Mama will torment me with questions about us."

Us? His heart jackhammered. "Then I'll check out your house, and your parents will never know I'm there."

She sighed. "Oh, all right. Can I at least change into my regular clothes?"

"If you must." He stood.

"I don't need an escort." She rolled her eyes. "The security guard is still here and the place is locked."

"Just work with me here." Mitch sat back down.

Something in her eyes softened. "I'll be right back."

Had she heard the desperation in his plea?

Seeing her again had stirred up every memory and feeling he thought he'd buried. He might be desperate to keep her safe, but he was just as desperate to win her love again.

Caitlyn changed out of her sequined rodeo queen outfit and into her own jeans and Western-themed T-shirt.

*I need a breather.* She leaned back against the wall. Deep, slow breaths. Get through the drive home, and tomorrow she'd figure out how to get rid of him. She'd even consider protective custody—as long as he wasn't the protector.

After a couple of minutes, she calmed down and dug

her lipstick from her oversize purse. No, he'd think she'd reapplied for him. She dropped the lipstick, smoothed her hair and straightened her shoulders. Ready for battle, she opened the dressing room door.

A man was leaning against the wall to her left.

She opened her mouth, but the scream died on her lips. Glen.

"Hey, it's me." He patted her shoulder.

"I didn't know you were still here."

"You didn't really think Bob would let me leave without making sure this place was locked up, did you? Did your friend leave?"

"He's not my friend. Just an old acquaintance." Understatement of the year.

"Oh." He shrugged. "Ready for me to escort you to your car?"

"Yes, please." She smiled. Mitch problem solved.

For tonight anyway.

Mitch rolled his neck muscles from side to side and scanned the office. American flag buntings decorated each window. As star spangled as Caitlyn's glitzy jacket and hat but without the sequins.

Stubborn woman. Hadn't changed a bit in the past ten years.

Except she was even more beautiful.

If anything happened to her, he'd die. How could he convince her to go into protective custody?

The muscles in the back of his neck ached and he massaged them as he paced.

Her dad. Yes. He'd go see her dad first thing in the morning. And Caitlyn would be in a safe house before she could say the word *no*.

As long as he made it to his sister's wedding, his family wouldn't be too upset. And surely by then, he'd have this case closed.

Nervous energy jolted through him. Out of all the people he'd vowed to protect over the years, he'd never had to protect someone he loved. He had to keep Caitlyn safe.

And she should be back by now. Mitch stepped into the hall.

No sign of movement. His heart pounded.

"Caitlyn." He hurried toward the dressing room.

"You're still here?" A man's voice behind him.

Mitch spun around.

The assistant he'd met earlier. Glen.

"Have you seen Caitlyn?"

"I escorted her to her car."

"You what?" Mitch's pulse went into overdrive.

"She came out of the dressing room." Glen frowned. "I was supposed to escort her to her car after the rodeo, so I asked if she was ready."

Something in his chest roiled. What if Glen was the stalker? What if he'd done something to Caitlyn? Mitch locked his best bad-cop glower on Glen. The man didn't flinch, didn't look away. Telling the truth.

"Did she go home?"

"I think she went to her store. Said something about needing her laptop."

"Where is her store?"

"Across the street a ways down, next to the Texas Cowboy Hall of Fame. It's called the Sassy Cowgirl/Rowdy Cowboy."

Mitch bolted for the door.

*Thanks, Mitch.* He'd successfully given Caitlyn a case of the creeps with his warnings that her stalker might be at her house. Now she was afraid to go home.

She shut and locked the office door, blocking the view

from the windowed showroom. No one could peer in and see her now. A shiver skittered up her spine and she sank into the chair at her desk.

At least she'd managed a few minutes to gather herself—for her hands to stop shaking, her heart to stop rattling, her brain to numb. Caitlyn closed her laptop and stuffed it in her oversize purse, then straightened the few items on her raw pine desk.

It was only a letter. Natalie, Bob and Mitch had all over-reacted. She wasn't some whimpering ninny. She'd taken self-defense classes. If anything happened, she could handle herself.

Just settle down. Her store—her dream—always settled her nerves.

Deep breaths. In and out. She was safe. Her stalker wasn't here. But if she didn't get moving, Mitch *would* trail her here. At the moment, she really wasn't sure which she feared more.

If she called him now, she'd end up riding with him. If she could just get brave enough to make a run for her car, then she could call and let him follow her.

She grabbed her keys, blew out a cleansing breath and pulled the back door open.

A man's large silhouette filled the doorway. "Hello, Camille. I've been waiting to get you alone."

# Chapter 2

Caitlyn screamed and dropped her purse. She stumbled back into her office and grabbed for the doorknob. Her hand met air.

"I told you I'd come for you." The man stepped inside and slammed the door behind him. Dark blond hair, gray-blue eyes, narrow face, no scars. She'd never seen him before. Lines deepened with his malevolent smile as he raised an open switchblade, stroking the edge with his thumb.

No mask. Her stomach jolted. He didn't plan on her escaping. Or maybe even surviving.

Why, oh, why, hadn't she let Mitch drive her home? She backed farther into the office.

The man's hand shot out toward her.

With a quick pivot around her desk, she made it to the showroom door. *Just get it open and lock him in the office.* Then maybe she could make it back to the coliseum before the man could get through the side alley and around front to catch up with her.

A rough hand clamped her left wrist and twisted her arm behind her back. She yelped. His knife-wielding hand snaked over her right shoulder. The cold blade scraped her throat. Would Mitch figure out where she was and come in time to save her? But what if he had already trailed her here? What if the man had hurt Mitch? Or worse? Her insides twisted.

"You're more of a fighter than you used to be. I like that." His hot breath fanned her neck.

A whiff of sour alcohol turned her stomach. "I'm not Camille. My name is Caitlyn."

"Did you really think you could change your name to Caitlyn Wentworth and I wouldn't recognize you? I'd know my Camille anywhere."

A shudder quaked through her. "You're hurting me."

The knife pressed against her neck, but he let go of her wrist. He smoothed her hair, and then wound it around his hand.

She gasped.

He wound tighter, jerking her head back.

Shock waves shot through her scalp. She bit her lip to keep from crying out.

"Now, let's turn around real slow and leave out the back way. If you scream, I'll cut any rescuer's throat. We're going home, Camille. You've played your game long enough."

Think. Think. She obviously couldn't convince this lunatic she wasn't Camille. She had to get away. *God, please help me. I don't mind dying, but not like this.*

The man shoved her toward the back door. With his hand still wound in her hair, she saw mostly ceiling.

"Can I get my purse?" Anything for a weapon.

"You don't need it. Drop the keys. You're leaving this life behind."

"At least let me lock up. If my purse is here and the store

is unlocked, police will suspect foul play." Play his game, keep him calm.

"I knew you were ready to come home." He pressed his lips against her ear. "All right, grab your purse and lock up."

Bile rose in her throat. She swallowed hard. "You can put the knife away. I'll go home with you."

"Not until we get there. You ran off once. I won't give you another chance." He stopped at the back door.

She felt around, found her purse and clutched it against her. With his left hand tangled deep in her hair, his right arm over her shoulder pressing the knife against her throat and the length of him against her back, she staggered outside.

One lone light drove the darkness from the still-dim parking area behind the store. No sign of Mitch. Or anyone else.

The man turned her so she could lock the door.

"I can't see. Can you loosen up on my hair a little?"

"You better not try nothing." His hand unwound a tiny bit.

"I have to lean down to see the lock and I'm afraid you'll accidentally cut me."

His arm was still over her shoulder, the heel of his hand resting above her chest, but she couldn't feel the cold steel on her throat any longer. The knife was still close. But it was now or never.

With all her might, she jabbed her right elbow back and met torso.

The man cursed. His grip around her neck let up. The knife sliced into her shoulder.

She spun and brought her knee up hard. With a groan, he bent double and fell between her and her car. She bolted around him.

A hand clamped around her ankle. Heat seared through her calf. Her shadow cast him in darkness. Blindly, she swung her heavy purse at him and stomped his arm with her free foot. He groaned and cursed. His hand fell away.

Caitlyn staggered for the car. Each step sent hot waves through her calf. She jerked the door open, fell inside and slammed the lock button down. She jabbed the key at the ignition but couldn't find it. The man stood. Her key finally hit the target and she revved the engine.

He darted in front of her car.

"Oh, God, help." She jammed her foot on the gas. The car lurched forward and the man dove out of the way.

"Thank You, Lord." She blew out a breath.

Tires squealing, she turned up the long alley between the building that housed her store and the Texas Cowboy Hall of Fame and then onto East Exchange. With the rodeo long over, the stores, restaurants and even bars had closed, leaving the main brick-lined street of the Fort Worth Stockyards abandoned.

Except for Mitch's SUV parked in front of her store.

As her vision tunneled, she shook her head. "Dear Lord, let him be all right. Help me."

She stomped the brake and her tires squealed as she lurched to a stop in front of Mitch. Woozy. Vision narrowing. She shook her head again and flung the door open.

"Caitlyn?"

*He's safe. Thank You, Lord.* She tried to slide out of her car. Her legs trembled.

A flashlight beam blinded her. She looked down to avoid the glare. Blood on the leg of her jeans. "I'm hurt."

"Caitlyn? What happened?" Mitch's panicked voice sounded a lot farther away than the glare of his light.

"We have to get out of here before he…" With her last ounce of strength she stood, but her legs didn't hold her. Strong arms encircled her. Arms she'd often dreamed of. Everything went black.

* * *

The antiseptic hospital smell singed Mitch's taste buds. He traced his fingers over Caitlyn's delicate cheekbone. Her even breath fanned his knuckles. The doctor had repaired the damage. Only sleeping now.

How long had it been since he'd thanked God for anything? But another inch and the puncture would have severed a major artery in her calf instead of only nicking it. Thank goodness she was alive and hadn't been sexually assaulted.

All moisture evaporated from his mouth. A bitter taste rose in his throat.

Where had her attacker been hiding? He never should have let her slip away from him. What would have happened if she hadn't escaped? What would he have done if he'd lost her? Again. Permanently this time.

All these years, as long as he'd known she was out there somewhere, he could go through the motions of life. How had he ever let her go? Her huge sapphire eyes, her curtain of dark tresses, her soft, inviting lips. Her stubbornness.

When she'd turned down his long-ago proposal, he should have slung her over his shoulder and taken her to Garland kicking and screaming.

He wouldn't let her go again. He'd find a way to win her love all over again. To convince her he'd stay safe. Especially if he got the transfer to forensics.

"I love you, Caitlyn." His lips grazed her soft cheek. "I always have."

Sapphire eyes fluttered open. She squinted at him. A tremulous smile.

Had she heard him? His heart revved. Did she still feel the same way?

But her smile melted away and she frowned. "What happened?"

"You were attacked. I called Natalie. She and your folks are on their way."

"My leg hurts."

"I'll call the nurse." He pressed the call button. "What do you remember?"

"He was waiting." She trembled. "In the alley behind my store when I left."

"Why did you leave the coliseum?"

"I didn't want to ride with you." She bit her lip. "But then I was afraid to go home. I was going to call you once I got back to my car and let you follow me."

Mitch's heart twisted. She'd put herself in danger to avoid him. "I knew I should have stuck closer to you. Did you see him?"

"Yes." She closed her eyes.

The door opened and a nurse stepped inside.

"She's hurting." Mitch moved back to allow the nurse access.

"I'll see what I can do." The nurse checked Caitlyn's chart.

As the nurse left, Caitlyn's parents entered, wide-eyed worry shining on their faces.

"Mr. Wentworth, nice seeing you again." Mitch stood and offered his hand to her dad.

Daniel Wentworth frowned. "Mitch? What are you doing here? What happened?"

"Oh, sweetie, what happened?" Claire Wentworth scurried to her daughter's side and took Caitlyn's hand in her own.

"Caitlyn was attacked, but the doctor said she'll be fine." Mitch tried to sound reassuring, though he was as worried about her as her folks were.

"Attacked?" Claire squeaked.

"I fought him off—thanks to that self-defense course

Daddy made me take. But I think he stabbed my leg. And maybe my shoulder?"

"A puncture wound to her left calf, but the knife only grazed her shoulder."

"So you're here working her mugging case?" Daniel's gaze pinned him.

"I'm on the case, sir. But I'm afraid this was no mugging. Your daughter received a threatening letter at Cowtown Coliseum."

The door flung open again and Natalie rushed into the room. "Caitlyn, are you all right?"

"I'm fine."

Natalie turned on Mitch. "How did this happen?"

"It's not Mitch's fault."

Oh, but it was. He should have known she'd try to slip out of his life. Just as she had ten years ago.

"It's that nut's fault." Natalie smoothed Caitlyn's hair. "I told you this was serious."

"You did." Caitlyn's chin trembled. "I should have listened."

"You knew about Caitlyn's letters." Daniel glared at his eldest daughter.

"I only found the latest one tonight." Natalie held both palms toward Daniel.

Daniel's eyebrows rose. "Why didn't you tell anyone, Caitlyn?"

*Because she figured I'd show up.*

"Mr. Wentworth, I know you're worried about Caitlyn, but I need to question her about what happened. And I need to get a description of her assailant while everything is still fresh in her memory."

"You want us to leave?" Daniel's how-dare-you tone sliced the air.

"I'm sorry, sir. Caitlyn was the victim of a violent crime. I need to get a statement and then I need you to help me convince her to go into protective custody until we get this guy."

"Absolutely not," Caitlyn snapped.

"In your protective custody?" Daniel growled.

The accusation was there in her father's eyes. Entrust her safety to the guy who'd broken her heart? The guy she'd gotten the drop on tonight?

He'd momentarily forgotten how slippery she could be. But it wouldn't happen again.

"I'll protect her with my life, sir. Now, I'm sorry, but I need to speak with Caitlyn."

"I won't leave until I know my daughter is safe." Daniel folded his arms across his chest the way Caitlyn did when she dug in her heels.

"There are two other rangers outside the room. Her name is on the hospital's top-secret list and visitors can't get to her without the code I gave only to Natalie. The sooner I get Caitlyn's description and take her statement, the sooner we can put her in protective custody. And the sooner we can ID the suspect, the sooner we can pick this guy up."

Caitlyn glared at him. "I'm not going into protective custody. I have two stores to run and I can't let the rodeo down."

"Marie is quite capable of taking care of both stores." Natalie settled on the foot of Caitlyn's bed. "I'll even help out if you need me to and Cowtown will understand. Besides, that's what the backup queens are for."

"How about this?" Mitch held her gaze. "Technically, I'm off for two weeks for my sister's wedding near San Antonio. Caitlyn could go with me. She'd be out of the line of fire and safe. But not necessarily in protective custody."

"No," Caitlyn wailed.

Daniel's eyebrows rose. "You were willing to give up your time off to take Caitlyn's case?"

"When I heard Caitlyn was in danger, I went back on duty."

"I think it's a good idea." Daniel's gaze sought his stubborn daughter's.

"Daddy!"

"I want you safe, pumpkin." Her dad pinned her with a don't-argue glare.

Caitlyn's mouth clamped shut.

"Now, I need the room cleared." Mitch opened the door.

"I'm trusting you—" Daniel turned toward Mitch "—to keep her safe, in spite of herself."

"You can count on it, sir." Caitlyn had already slipped through his fingers. Twice. It wouldn't happen again.

"I don't want y'all to go." Caitlyn's voice cracked.

"We'll be right outside, pumpkin." Daddy kissed her forehead and exited.

Mama hugged her, then followed, and Natalie squeezed her shoulder.

"Don't tell them what the letters said," Caitlyn whispered. "They don't need all the details to worry about."

Natalie nodded and left her alone with Mitch.

The taupe walls of the tiny hospital room seemed to close in on her, stealing her breath.

Could this nightmare get any worse?

Had he said he loved her when she woke up? Or had she dreamed it? Or imagined it?

"Now, tell me everything you remember about the attack and the assailant." He pulled a chair near her bed and opened his sketch pad.

"You're drawing him?"

"You always said I should do something with my art." He grinned.

"Then what? Put his sketch on TV like the Unabomber?"

"Maybe. But first I'll compare the sketch to our database

of violent offenders and come up with a lineup to see if you can identify him before we head to Medina."

"That's where your grandfather lives, right?" Approximately five hours in his SUV. Alone with Mitch. A tremor shook all the way down to her soul.

"That's right. Caitlyn, I need you to focus. We need to get this guy off the streets."

If they could catch him, she'd be safe. Her life could go back to normal. A normal Mitchless, stalkerless life.

She closed her eyes, cleared her mind and concentrated on what had happened at her store. "I opened the back door and he was there. He said, 'Hello, Camille. I've been waiting to get you alone.'" She shivered.

"Describe his voice."

"Hoarse. A smoker's voice. Gravelly."

"Then what happened?"

"I backed into the store and tried to lock him out, but he got inside. He was thin, a couple inches shorter than you. Maybe six-one."

Why did everything always come back to him?

"Which hand did he hold the knife in?"

"Right."

An accurate description would get Mitch out of her life. Just the way she liked him. Ten years since he'd chosen a dangerous job over her. Why couldn't her heart let go?

A face took shape on Mitch's sketch pad as Caitlyn described her attacker. His chest burned. What he'd like to do to this guy—

Concentrate. Effectively capture the suspect's features. "Age?"

"Maybe fifty."

It all depended on Caitlyn's memory. And she'd been distracted by her family. His fault, but he knew how close-knit they were and how worried her parents were.

A few more details and he turned the pad toward Caitlyn. Her eyes widened. "It's close. Really close."

"What should I change?"

"His cheekbones. They were higher. His skin seemed like it was pulled tight. Lips a little thinner. His eyes were sleepy looking. And his forehead was higher, with a receding hairline."

A very detailed description. Just let it be accurate.

As Mitch erased a few lines and started sketching again, a heavy-lidded man emerged with a high hairline. He worked on the lips and cheekbones next, then turned the sketch for Caitlyn to see again.

She gasped. "That's him."

# Chapter 3

"**Y**ou're sure?" Mitch held the sketch steady. They had to catch this guy fast. He had to keep her safe. "I don't need to change anything else?"

Caitlyn examined the face on the pad. "That's him. Almost an exact likeness." She shivered again. "Can my family come back now?"

"I need you to agree to the trip to Medina or protective custody. One or the other."

"Maybe it won't come to that. Maybe you'll ID him tonight and he'll be in jail tomorrow."

"I hope so. But if not?"

A heavy sigh escaped her. "Does protective custody have to involve you?"

"I can keep you safe, Caitlyn."

"I'm sure there are other officers."

"Yes, but they don't know you." Or love you. "I've got more at stake."

She frowned.

*Might as well tell her, while she's awake, that you never stopped loving her, Warren.* "If I let anything happen to you, your dad would kill me." Nice save.

A grin tugged at the corner of her mouth, but her shoulders slumped. "Door number one. I'd love to see your family and be there for Tara's wedding. She actually sent me an invitation."

"Were you planning to go?"

"No."

"Why?"

"Because I knew you'd be there." She shrugged.

Trying to avoid him because she didn't love him anymore. But now she was stuck with him. Might as well take advantage of his good fortune. Could he win her back?

"I've thought about you a lot over the years."

Her hand sliced through the air as if she were a director shouting *cut*. "Don't even go there."

"I…"

"I'll go to Medina on one condition."

"What's that?"

"We don't discuss us."

"All right." His gaze dropped to the floor.

"When will we leave?"

"Tomorrow evening. The doctor wants to keep you for observation until then."

"I'd like to see my family now."

"Of course."

"Without you lurking." Caitlyn bit her lip.

His heart twisted. "I'll be right outside."

While Caitlyn's family visited with her, Mitch sat in the chair outside her door. He scanned the database against his sketch and her description, then pasted every possible match into a file.

A familiar face popped up on the laptop screen. His

breath stalled. A dead ringer for his sketch. If Caitlyn's memory was accurate, this guy could be his break in the case. Stuart Stevens. A tap on the mouse opened Stevens's criminal record and Mitch read the first page. A long list of domestic disturbances. A wife—Cammie.

Mitch's heart jolted. Cammie. Camille.

Cammie had borne various bruises over the years, but every time neighbors called the police, she refused to admit her husband had caused her injuries. Mitch flipped through more pages.

The domestic disturbances ended twelve years ago. A long gap until nine months ago—an arrest for beating his eighteen-year-old son, Trent. Charges pressed. Stevens had spent five months in jail and gotten paroled two months ago. Then disappeared from the radar screen only weeks later.

There was a footnote with Trent's current address at Texas A&M. Emergency contact—Quinn Remington.

Mitch knew that name. The man his parents had sold the family horse ranch to when they'd moved to Denton. Small world.

Searching through suspects, Mitch pasted several more mug shots into the lineup to complete it and then snapped the laptop shut.

Maybe he wouldn't be taking Caitlyn to Medina after all. His heart hitched. Not that he wanted her in danger. He just wanted the excuse to be near her. If the case was over, she'd skitter out of his life as fast as she'd skittered in.

"Salvo." He approached Ranger Salvo at his post in the hall. "I'm going back in."

"I'm on it." Salvo took Mitch's spot at the door.

Mitch knocked. "It's me."

"Come in."

Was that hesitation in her voice? He stepped inside her room.

Her mom and sister perched on each side of her narrow bed, with her dad in a chair at her feet.

"I have a lineup I want you to take a look at."

"Sure." Caitlyn reached for the laptop.

The women moved out of the way and Mitch scooted a chair beside her bed to watch the screen and her reactions. Stevens was on the third page.

She scanned the first page and shook her head. "He's not here."

A tap of his mouse pulled up the next screen.

"No." She sighed.

The next page popped up.

Seconds passed. No reaction. Her breath caught.

"What…" Her dad stood.

Mitch raised his hand to silence her dad.

"That's him." Caitlyn pointed toward the bottom of the screen. Her hand shook.

"Which one?"

"This one." Her finger hovered close to Stuart Stevens's face.

"You're sure?"

"Positive."

"You did great." Mitch scooped the laptop away from her and laid his hand on her arm. She trembled. "It's okay, now. You're safe." He pushed his chair back in the corner.

Her mom and sister reclaimed their spots on her bed, patting and soothing.

If only he could be the one to comfort her.

Maybe his dead-on sketch of Stevens would land him the forensics position. And he could be Caitlyn's lifelong comforter.

Mitch stepped back out into the hall and pulled up the number for headquarters.

"Timmons."

"Warren here. I've got an ID on Caitlyn Wentworth's

attacker. Check Stuart Stevens's prints against the letters and envelopes and I want an APB on him."

"You got it."

"Keep me updated." Mitch ended the call and dialed the number for Remington Horse Ranch.

"Remington Ranch."

"Quinn, it's Mitch Warren."

"What can I do you for?"

"I'm working a case involving Stuart Stevens."

Quinn sighed. "What'd he do now?"

"Assault with a deadly weapon. Thought Trent might be able to help us."

"He's home for the weekend. Just a minute."

Silence for a few seconds.

"Hello?" The young man's voice was filled with dread.

"This is Ranger Mitch Warren. I'm afraid your dad's gotten into some trouble, son."

"Assault with a deadly weapon." The boy sounded as if nothing his father did surprised him. "Quinn told me. Who did he hurt? Are they okay?"

"I can't get into the details, but the victim is out of danger." Mitch's jaw tensed. Poor kid. "Do you have any idea where your father is?"

"I haven't seen him since he went to jail." Trent blew out a shaky breath. "His parole officer's looking for him, too."

"I'm sorry, son. I know this must be hard on you."

"I'll do anything to keep him from hurting anyone else."

Mitch pinched the bridge of his nose. "You wouldn't happen to have a picture of your mom, would you?"

"An old one. Why? Did he hurt my mom again?"

"No. But it might help with the case. I'll send a ranger to get it."

"Sure, if it'll help. But I want it back."

"Of course. I appreciate your cooperation, son. I need you to tell me everything you can about your dad. Former addresses. Family. Friends. Where he hangs out. Places he's worked. Everything."

Anything. Anything that might keep Caitlyn safe.


Even though Caitlyn had slept through the night and most of the day, grogginess still tugged at her. She rubbed her bleary eyes. The pain pills worked wonders on her leg, but left her in a daze. And she needed all her faculties to deal with Mitch for the next five hours.

"Two weeks," Mama moaned. "That's a lifetime."

It did seem like a lifetime.

"Don't make it any worse on her." Daddy squeezed her hand. "Two weeks is nothing. And it probably won't take that long. She'll be home before we know it."

"But it seems like we just got Nattie back and now Caitie's leaving."

Caitlyn tried for a brave smile. "It's only two weeks, Mama." Mama had prayed for years for Natalie to return to the fold. Now that she had, Mama reveled in both of them being near.

"And we want Caitlyn safe." Natalie settled on the foot of her bed.

"Definitely." Daddy's eyes were too shiny.

"I'll be fine. I probably won't even have to go. Maybe they've caught him by now and it's all over."

A knock sounded and the door opened a crack.

Caitlyn tensed.

"Can I come in?" Mitch's voice came through the opening.

"Yes." She relaxed. Okay, she had to admit, he did make her feel safe.

The door swung open. Mitch stuffed both hands in his pockets. "Sorry, but we need to get Caitlyn out of here. Her decoy is here."

"Decoy?" Her life had become a cop show.

"A female officer similar in build and coloring. She wore a disguise here. You'll wear the disguise out. Just in case."

"They haven't caught him?"

"Not yet. But his prints are on all six letters and envelopes, so we've got a positive ID."

"What if they arrest him tonight?" She knew all of her panic echoed in her tone. Did he realize how desperate she was to escape spending any time with him?

"We've got an APB out on him, but his last known address is abandoned. We may not catch up with him quickly. He knows you can identify him, so he'll probably lay low."

"But surely he has enough sense not to hang out at the hospital."

"How sensible was he when he attacked you? And he may need medical attention after you stomped his arm." Mitch set a duffel bag on the chair near the foot of her bed. "Here, put these on. Get your mom or Natalie to help so you don't put too much weight on that leg. I'll be right outside."

"But why are we still going to Medina when he could be arrested any minute?"

"Until that jail cell clangs shut behind this guy, you're in danger." Daddy helped her stand and gave her a big hug. "You'll be fine, pumpkin. Mitch will keep you safe."

She blinked away tears and resisted the urge to cling to him as she had when she was a little girl.

Worry shone bright in Daddy's eyes as Mitch ushered him from the room.

Natalie dumped the contents of the bag on the bed. A short, curly gray wig and a shapeless housedress.

"Really?" Caitlyn shook her head.

"It's for your protection, Caitie." Mama held the dress out for her. "Nobody will recognize Ms. Cowgirl Couture in this. That's for sure."

"This is so not necessary."

"We think it is. Two against one." Natalie gathered Caitlyn's hair into a ponytail and plopped the wig on her head.

"And you— I've got a rhinestone to pick with you." Caitlyn jabbed a finger at her sister.

"I didn't break my promise." Natalie held up both palms. "All I did was tell Bob because I wanted you safe. He called the police. Not me."

"That's a technicality." Caitlyn rolled her eyes and settled on the side of the bed to wriggle the dress over her shorts and T-shirt. "And now I'm stuck with him."

"But you'll be safe. That's all that matters." Mama helped her find the sleeves. "Nattie did the right thing."

The bright zippered dress pulled a moan from Caitlyn. She'd never wear something like this in a million, trillion years. Maybe if she pretended to be an elderly grandmother she could deal with five hours in the car with Mitch. She shook her head as his chiseled jaw came to mind. No, not even imagining herself as an old lady would save her now.

Mitch scanned the hospital corridor. No one suspicious. No Stuart Stevens. Salvo was stationed outside Caitlyn's door.

The business suit fit perfectly, but he sure was glad he didn't have to wear one on a daily basis. Especially the tie. His fingers flexed, longing to tug it looser. The fake beard and mustache itched. His head felt downright naked without his cowboy hat.

His cell buzzed. Headquarters. "Warren here."

"It's Timmons. I forwarded you a picture of Trent Stevens's mom. You'll want to see it. I pulled up Caitlyn's head shot on the Cowtown website. The resemblance is amazing."

"Thanks." Mitch opened his email and tapped the attachment.

A sad-eyed Caitlyn stared back at him. His jaw dropped.

The woman looked so much like Caitlyn, they could be sisters. Could there be a family connection to explain the resemblance?

Beside the carbon copy of Caitlyn was a heavy-lidded man with dark blond hair. A younger Stuart Stevens. He'd follow up on who the woman was later. Right now, Caitlyn's safety was his only concern.

As he headed toward Caitlyn's room, Salvo scanned Mitch, put his hand on his holster and blocked the door. Recognition dawned in his eyes and he stepped aside. "Had me there for a minute."

"Good job." Mitch clapped him on the back and knocked on Caitlyn's door. "It's me."

"Come in," Natalie called.

A collective gasp escaped the women when they saw him.

"Relax. It's me."

The blue hair in the granny dress surrounded by Caitlyn's family barely resembled Caitlyn. But he'd know that blush anywhere.

"Let's get you home, Granny." Mitch offered his arm. "Doc says you're on the mend."

Her face went crimson. She slapped his arm. "Stop it."

"Just playing my role." Caitlyn looked cute, even dressed up like an old lady. He could happily grow old with her. He shook his head. Focus on keeping her safe.

In a few minutes, he'd hold in his hands the life of the woman he'd loved since high school. *God, help me keep her safe.*

Twice now. He'd acknowledged God's existence twice in one day. For the first time in a year.

"Are you driving all the way tonight?" Daniel checked his watch. "It'll be midnight by the time you get there. You must be tired."

"I grabbed some shut-eye and tanked up on coffee. I'll

stop at a hotel if I get too tired. Don't worry. I'll take good care of her."

"You'd better." Daniel nodded. "Sorry I was kind of gruff with you earlier."

"You were worried."

"Me, too." Natalie looked at the floor. "I was downright rude."

"The least of my problems."

"Can we have a minute with Caitlyn?" Claire asked.

"Sure. I'll wait outside."

The door opened and a nurse entered with a wheelchair. "Release papers."

"Thank you." Caitlyn accepted them.

"I know your young man is relieved." She turned her smile on Mitch. "He's barely left your side."

"He's not…"

"I'm a cop."

"Oh. I could have sworn you were a man in love. Silly me."

Mitch's ears heated and he glanced at Caitlyn. Their gazes met, but she quickly looked away. A stranger could see straight through him, but Caitlyn didn't see it or didn't care. Probably the latter.

"I'll be right outside. Just let me know when you're ready."

Two weeks to change her mind.


Caitlyn tried to fasten her seat belt, but she couldn't see around the huge dress to find the buckle. When she turned sideways, the bandage on her shoulder pulled. She winced.

"Let me help you." Mitch's hands grazed hers then worked at her hip.

By the time the belt clicked into place, his nearness had turned her into a bundle of nerves. "Why do old women wear this stuff?"

"Once we get down the road and I make sure no one's following, you can slip it off." He started the engine.

"And the wig?" She scratched at it.

"Patience." He grabbed her hand. "We can't be too cautious."

"I wasn't taking it off." She jerked her hand away. "It itches."

"So does my beard."

She inhaled the new-car smell of the Jeep. "Is this yours?"

"No. Belongs to the department."

*Concentrate on the situation instead of him.* "Tell me about the break in the case. Who is this guy?"

"Official business."

"Isn't the victim entitled to know about her attacker?"

Mitch checked his rearview mirror and merged into interstate traffic. "His son is working with us to help us find him."

"Wow, trying to get his own father arrested?"

"His dad beat his mom for years. She left twelve years ago and he turned his rage on his son. The son finally turned him in and his dad spent time in jail."

"She just left her son there?"

"This guy threatened to kill them both if she tried to take the kid." He checked his rearview mirror and covered her hand with his. "Her name is Cammie."

"Cammie. Camille." Caitlyn's insides quaked. "What's the man's name?"

"Stuart Stevens. The kid, Trent, had a picture of his dad and mom from fifteen years ago. She's a dead ringer for you."

"So why can't I go home?" She moistened her suddenly dry lips.

"You know they have no idea where he's been staying or where to find him."

"But if they catch up with him tonight, what then?"

"Then I'll drive you home tomorrow. Like it or not, you're stuck with me, Caitlyn. At least for the night."

But she did like it. That was the problem. She enjoyed having Mitch near.

And his family. She'd always loved them like her own. "How is your family? I don't see them much since they sold the ranch and moved to Denton."

"Mom and Dad are enjoying early retirement. But I think they miss the peacefulness of Aubrey. They're thinking about moving to Medina and helping Grandpa with his ranch. Tara and her fiancé are still in Dallas and Cody's still riding bulls on the circuit."

"Mr. Never-Grow-Up-and-Settle-Down—that's your brother."

"You'll love Medina. Very small town. A lot like Aubrey. No crime. You'll be safe."

Safe with Mitch. She could get used to that way too easily.

Lightning flashed, thunder boomed and Caitlyn slept.

Mitch gulped another swig of coffee and kept driving. Whatever they'd given her was obviously working. Just a few more miles and he'd arrive at the ranch.

Wind whipped at his SUV. Why did it have to be hurricane season? Medina never got storms except when he needed to see to drive at midnight.

All these years and his feelings hadn't changed—they'd grown stronger. Obviously not the case for her. Her main intent seemed to be avoiding him.

The rain intensified and he turned the wipers up to full blast.

Okay, he'd hurt her. He'd refused to give up his dream of following in his grandfather's footsteps to become a Texas Ranger. Why couldn't he have his dream and Caitlyn, too?

Why couldn't she see that after ten years in his chosen dangerous profession, he was still here?

Sure, there'd been a few scrapes over the years. His stomach turned. On and off the job. A year ago, it should have been him in that coffin instead of his partner. He'd often wished it had been.

But if it had gone down that way, he wouldn't be here to keep Caitlyn safe.

Mitch focused on the slick road and tried to clear his mind. Another torrent of water slammed the windshield. He almost couldn't see the yellow line, but with no other cars on the road, he crept along. His turn should be coming up.

Lightning flashed and he caught a glimpse of the iron gate. He almost missed it but managed the turn at the last possible moment. He rolled down the window and punched in the combination.

The electric gate slowly slid open. Caitlyn didn't stir as he drove down the narrow gravel drive to his grandfather's ranch. Dark shapes of cattle were barely visible past the fence lining both sides of the drive. There was something in his path ahead. His breath caught. A huge tree lay across the narrow road. He hit the brakes and slid in the muck.

Caitlyn screamed.

# Chapter 4

The Jeep slid into a ditch. Caitlyn jostled back and forth until they slammed to a halt, with the bumper lodged in an embankment.

"You okay?" Mitch turned toward her in the dim glow of the dash light.

"Fine." She sucked in a deep breath. "Just scared me."

"Rough way to wake up. Sorry about that. There's a tree blocking the road and I didn't have it in four-wheel drive."

"Where are we?"

"My grandfather's ranch, but we'll have to walk from here. It's not far. I'll carry you."

"I can walk."

"I'm sure you can. But Doc said to take it easy on your leg and keep it dry. Conditions aren't good for either precaution. Sit tight. I'll come around and get you."

Caitlyn opened her door and stepped out. Her foot sank in muck up to the ankle. She didn't care. Mitch would not carry her.

"Hey, wait up."

Within seconds, she was soaked through. Her bad leg had sunk deeper in the mire.

His hands settled on her shoulders.

"Please don't carry me." Her voice sounded small and vulnerable to her ears.

"At least lean on me." Mitch sighed. "Hop on your good leg."

His arm came around her shoulder, hers around his waist. Still too close. She hopped, expending much more energy than she had.

"You're splashing mud all over the place." He scooped her up before she could protest.

"No." She pushed against his chest with both hands.

"Don't fight me. It's not far." Mitch stepped over the fallen tree as if she weighed nothing.

Unshed tears singed. She was in Mitch's arms again. The way he would have carried her over the threshold if they'd gotten married. She pressed her face against his shoulder and let the tears roll.

"Shh, it's gonna be okay. I promise."

No, it would never be okay again. In two short days, Mitch had reawakened all the feelings she'd ever had for him—reopened the wound she'd worked so hard at healing. A wound that ran a lot deeper than the one on her leg.

Mitch could handle a lot of things. Dead bodies, crime scenes, bullets flying, but Caitlyn's tears weren't on the list. He cradled her against him. Heat surged through his chest. He'd rip Stuart Stevens apart with his bare hands.

"It's okay. We're here now." He climbed the porch steps.

"Put me down." She swiped at her eyes and pushed against him.

"No." He knocked on the door.

"I look like a drowned rat. At least let me walk in on my own two feet."

In the glow of the porch light, her hair hung in wet rivulets, her makeup mostly gone, her eyes red and swollen. Beautiful. His gaze settled on her lips. What he wouldn't give to kiss her.

She struggled against him.

"Stop wiggling." He tightened his grip. "I'm not putting you down until we're inside and dry. That leg's had enough trauma already."

"You'll feel the trauma if you don't put me down."

The door swung open. His mother scanned them both and her eyes lit up.

"Mitch. Caitlyn." Mom clasped her hands together. "She's your surprise guest. You finally married her!"

"Mom." His voice cracked. A wave of heat swept up his face. "No."

His mother's face fell. "Well, you're carrying her over the threshold."

"Caitlyn's hurt."

"What happened?" Mom stepped aside.

"I'll explain later." He strode into the foyer. Rain puddled at his feet on the hardwood flooring.

"If you don't put me down, I'm gonna hurt you," Caitlyn said with a note of warning in her tone.

Gently, he set her down, keeping his arm around her for support.

"Oh." His mother frowned. "I guess from the sounds of things, y'all aren't back together?"

"No, Mom. But don't tell anyone Caitlyn is here."

"I'm sorry, Audra." Caitlyn pushed wet strands of hair away from her face. "I should be more grateful for Mitch's help. It's nice to see you again. I'd hug you, but I can barely stand and I'm all wet."

"Of course, dear, let's get you settled and dry. I put new sheets on in the guest room."

Caitlyn hobbled beside him, clinging to his waist. At least she needed him.

As they neared the staircase, she stopped. "Upstairs?"

"Sorry, the only bedroom down here is Grandpa's." His mother wrung her hands. "I didn't know you were hurt. We can move Grandpa upstairs."

"No, really. It's fine." Caitlyn limped toward the stairs. "It'll be good exercise for me."

"The only other option is my cabin." Mitch bore her slight weight with each step she took. "We could stay there."

"No." Her refusal came quick.

"Then let me carry you."

With a sigh, her shoulders sagged. "Tonight. But after that, hands off."

"Deal." He scooped her up to find her stiff this time, not soft and clingy as she'd been outside. And as soon as he hit the top step, she pushed against him.

"Need me to help?" His mother called up the stairs.

"I can manage," Caitlyn called back. "Go on to bed. Sorry to keep you up so late."

Unwillingly, he set her down. "It's right here. First door to the right."

They made halting steps with Caitlyn leaning on him again in slow progress to the guest room. "So your mom has no clue what's going on?"

"No. I thought it would be better to fill them all in once we got here rather than take the chance that Stuart Stevens knows how to hack into cell phones."

She shuddered. "You think he might?"

"There's nothing in his file to suggest it, but it never hurts to be too careful." With each step, she leaned more heavily against him. "I got you a new cell and one for each of your family members, all under accounts with

fake names. That way, you can call them without having
to worry. And keep tabs on your store through Natalie. I
know that's important to you."

Caitlyn looked up at him. "Thanks."

"No problem." They finally made it to the guest room
and he helped her settle in a chair.

"Need Mom to help you change?"

"I think I could manage if I had something to change
into."

"Right." He ran his hand along the back of his neck.
"I left the bag your mom put together for you in the Jeep.
Mom'll come up with something. I'll send her up, then be
back to check on you."

"You don't have to check on me. I'm fine."

Obviously she didn't want to bother his mom, but she
wanted him hovering near even less. "Maybe I want to."
He shot her a wink, watched her cheeks pink and closed
the door.

"Does she need anything?" Mom waited in the hall.

"Something to sleep in. Her bag's in the Jeep and there's
a tree across the driveway where the cattle guard used to
be. That's why we were so wet."

"I'm on it." She turned toward her and his father's room.
"You go on downstairs."

Exhaustion dragged at his legs as he descended the
stairs. He wanted to go to his room, stay close to Caitlyn,
but he had to clue his mother in first.

He sat in front of the fireplace with no flame in sight—
his mother's favorite spot even in the heat of summer. With
the chill of his damp clothes, a fire would be nice about
now, even though it was only mid-September. Two cups
of coffee, with steam swirling, waited on the end table between the two wooden rockers. He chose the darker brew,
cradling the smooth porcelain in his hands.

Coffee this time of night was nothing. His family often

joked about caffeine running through their veins instead of blood.

A few minutes later, Mom descended the stairs and settled in the chair beside him.

"She okay?"

"I ran her a bath so she can get warm."

"Can she handle that? She's not supposed to get her stitches wet."

"I hope so. She ran me out."

"I'll check on her in a bit." Mitch sipped his coffee. Strong and dark, just the way he liked it. "I can't believe all our commotion didn't wake Grandpa up."

"He helped drive the longhorns to the north pasture today, so he turned in early. You know how hard he sleeps, especially when he's tired." Mom's oak chair creaked with each rock. "What's going on, Mitch? Caitlyn's in danger, isn't she?"

"How did you know that?"

Mom held up one finger. "She doesn't seem to be here willingly." A second finger went up. "You don't want anyone knowing she's here, and she said you were helping her." A third finger completed the list.

"We're all safe."

"That's not what worries me. I can tell she's shaken, and you know I always loved that girl."

"Yeah, me, too."

"Oh, Mitch." Mom reached for his hand. "Can't y'all work it out?"

"Right now, I have to keep her safe, and that's all I can think about." He clasped her hand. "Some nut thinks she's his estranged wife. He's been stalking her and he attacked her the other night."

Mom's free hand flew to her heart.

"Outside of this family, no one can know she's here."

"Of course. You're sure he didn't follow you here?"

"I'm sure. But we can't do anything to lead him here. I'll fill Grandpa in tomorrow and as the others arrive, I'll brief them." He dug his phone out of his pocket. "I need to call her dad."

"At this hour?"

"He said to call when we got here, no matter what time. You go on to bed."

She stood and patted his knee. "Well, I'm glad you brought her here."

"Me, too."

For this short period in his life, Caitlyn needed him. He'd wring everything he could out of it before time ran out.

Maybe if his transfer came through, their time wouldn't run out.


Caitlyn winced and tried to pull herself up with her good arm. Nothing. She'd had to take a bath so she could prop her leg on the side of the deep claw-foot tub and keep it dry. But now she couldn't get out. She would not call Mitch's mom. She'd always loved Mitch's mom, but she wouldn't even want her own mother fishing her out of the tub.

White-lace curtains and pale yellow walls created a soothing place for a bubble bath. Maybe another day she'd run one when it wasn't so late and she wasn't so exhausted.

Summoning all her strength, she tried again. Her hand slid on the white-tiled surround, but she managed to perch on the side of the tub with her bad leg out and her good leg in. Exhausted, she sat there gasping deep breaths until her heart slowed, then pulled her good leg out of the tub.

Red swelling ran along one edge of the wound. Probably infected from all the mud she'd sloshed through tonight. Leaning her weight on her good leg, she stood and dried off.

Shoulder throbbing, she slid the cotton gown Audra had supplied over her head and stuck her arms through the sleeves. She hobbled to the linen closet and opened the door, searching for peroxide. The familiar brown bottle with a spray nozzle hid behind extra toilet paper and shampoo.

White foam bubbled up as she sprayed, and it stung. She shut the toilet lid, sat down and blew on it like her mom used to do when she was little. After a few minutes, she dabbed the wound dry, hobbled out of the bathroom and crawled into bed.

How could the simple act of bathing and dressing be so taxing? There were people in the world who lived with disabilities that made every effort exhausting. Her injuries were temporary. Her situation was temporary. Mitch in her life was temporary.

Count every blessing. Especially that Mitch was temporary.

A knock sounded on her door. "Caitlyn, can I come in?"

Speak of the temporary blessing.

"I'm fine."

"Can I come in?"

He sure made it hard to count blessings. She propped a mound of pillows behind her and pulled the covers higher. "If you must."

The door opened and she closed her eyes.

"How's your leg?"

"Fine."

"Really?"

"I kept it dry. I cleaned it and sprayed it with peroxide."

"Are you okay?" The tender caring in his tone tugged at her.

"I'm fine. Just really tired."

"I don't see why. It's only two-fifteen in the morning." His grin echoed in his voice. "The second night this week I've kept you out till all hours."

"I need to call my family. They'll be worried."

"I already did. Your dad said to call no matter what time we arrived. Lay down."

Too tired to argue, she pushed the pillows aside and scooted down in the bed.

"Get some rest." Mitch tucked the covers under her chin—his fingers grazed her cheek. "But if you need anything, I'm right next door."

Her eyes flew open—wide-awake. The door closed and she could hear soft footfalls in the next room, the shower running and finally the creak of bedsprings. His mere proximity would keep her awake for hours. Even with a wall between them and the downpour they'd tramped through, she could still smell his cologne. And feel his touch.

No response. Mitch knocked on her door again, then opened it. "Caitlyn."

Nothing. He peered into the darkened room, his eyes adjusting to the dimness. Still sleeping. She'd barely even changed position. Obviously she needed the rest.

He closed the door and headed downstairs.

Poor Grandpa had tramped down to the ranch entrance to cut up the tree this morning. At least the rain had stopped and the sun had popped out of the overcast clouds. The distant whir of the chain saw made him feel guilty, but he couldn't leave Caitlyn.

The smell of bacon wafted from the kitchen with the clang of Mom's pots and pans. The large house still had a cozy feel, with Grandma Lyla's quilts displayed in every room, the rich, cedar-paneled walls and down-home furnishings.

Tara should arrive any minute. His little sister—getting married. At least they all approved of her fiancé.

Gravel crunched in the drive. Mitch pushed the sheer curtain aside to get a better look. Tara. He charged out the door to meet her.

By the time he'd jogged to her car, she'd unloaded a suitcase. But four more were jammed in the trunk.

"Let me help you with those. Did you bring your whole closet?"

"Mitch." She set down her case and hugged him. "I'm so glad we're all such movers and shakers that we can take two weeks off to spend together before my wedding. What more could a girl ask for?"

He gently bonked her nose. "I'm glad you're so happy. No cold feet?"

"Not even a pinky toe."

"How's the hair-salon business?" He picked up three cases.

"Thriving."

"Seriously, sis, do you really need all this stuff?"

"Two weeks of clothing, plus my wedding trousseau. I thought I'd packed light."

"Trousseau?"

Tara shook her head and linked her arm through his baggage-laden elbow. "So tell me—any women in your life?"

His breath stalled.

"I knew it." She pointed a finger at him. "It's that Raquel, isn't it? She seemed really sweet and her son is a little charmer."

"How many times do I have to tell you?" Mitch shook his head. "There's nothing between Raquel and me. I'm merely trying to help her out and give Hunter a male presence in his life."

"You still feel guilty, don't you?"

"Why shouldn't I? Her husband—her five-year-old son's father—is dead. Because of me."

"Mitch." She sighed. "Dylan died because he fell asleep at the wheel."

"Yes, but I knew he was tired. I was his partner and I didn't have his back that night."

"You offered to wait and drive him home, but he said

he was fine." She patted his arm as they climbed the porch steps. "Have you ever thought that maybe Dylan died that night because it was God's timing for him to go home?"

"Pondered on it." *Told Him I didn't like His timing. We haven't spoken much since.*

The front door swung open. Mom did a little bounce. "Tara, you're here."

Nice rescue. He really didn't want to get into what he thought about God's rotten timing. Or what God thought of him questioning it.

She ushered them inside and Mitch headed for the stairs. "I'll take these on up and check on Caitlyn before I get the rest of your suitcases."

"Caitlyn?" Tara's eyebrows rose. "As in Caitlyn Wentworth?"

"It's not what you think." Mitch set the suitcases down. "It's work. She's in danger. I'll fill you in after I get your car unloaded. But as far as anyone outside this family is concerned, she's not here."

"You're scaring me."

"She's safe. We all are. The nut after her has no idea where she is, but we can't be too careful."

"Of course. Not a word."

He picked up the cases again and ascended the stairs. The fifth and eighth steps creaked, as they had since he could remember.

An odd sound, like a puppy bark, came from Caitlyn's room.

"What was that?" Tara pressed a hand to her heart.

"Caitlyn!" Mitch left the suitcases and took the rest of the stairs two at a time. He shouldn't have left her alone. Had Stevens found her?

He topped the stairs and flung her door open without knocking. She lay in a heap beside her bed. Unconscious. He scanned the room.

No one else here.

Her breathing was soft, but her face was flushed. Mitch pressed a gentle palm to her cheek. Too warm. His heart lurched.

"Caitlyn!" She didn't move. "Caitlyn!"

Gently, he touched her uninjured shoulder, shaking her. Her skin heated his fingers.

A moan escaped her dry lips.

"Tara! Call Stan!"

# Chapter 5

Chilled to the bone, Caitlyn shivered as her teeth chattered. Dreaming of Mitch again. But even in her dreams, he'd walked out on her. Again. She tried to call out to him, but her tongue lodged in her dry mouth and no sound came. If she could just open her eyes…but weights seemed to sit on each eyelid.

Hot, so hot. Her leg was on fire. What had she done to it? And her temples throbbed. She pushed at the covers.

A hand touched her cheek. "Her fever's breaking." Mitch's voice from far away.

"Good. I've cleaned the wound. Once she wakes, I'll give her a shot to combat the infection and make sure she doesn't have a concussion." Another male voice. But she didn't know this one.

She opened her eyes.

Mitch's face. Close to hers.

"Hey." He smiled down at her.

Was she dreaming again? No—she could feel his hand on her cheek. "Hey."

"Feeling better?"

"I'm burning up." Her eyes wouldn't stay open. She pressed a hand to her forehead. Sweat soaked and clammy.

"You were, but your fever broke."

She tried to roll to her side. White-hot heat shot through her calf. Her eyes flew open.

Muted sea-foam walls…matched Mitch's eyes. White curtains and handmade quilt. Farmhouse furnishings.

Mitch's grandpa's ranch.

Stalker.

The knife.

An older man stood next to Mitch. Gray hair. Not his dad. Or his grandfather.

"This is Dr. Stan Adams, Mom's cousin. I had Tara call him."

"You gave Mitch quite a scare, Miss Wentworth." The man smiled, putting her at ease. "How are you feeling?"

"Weak. I tried to get up, but I was dizzy."

"You hit your head on the nightstand when you fell, and your leg wound is infected." The doctor shone a flashlight in each eye. "No signs of concussion. I'll give you a shot and leave antibiotics with Mitch. Are you allergic to anything?"

"Penicillin."

"That rules out a lot of drugs. Is there any chance you could be pregnant?"

"I've never…" Her face heated even more. She clamped her lips shut and glanced at Mitch.

He grinned at her.

"No. Absolutely no chance." Her face scalded.

"All right, then. Are you taking any medication other than pain pills?"

"No."

"Arm or…" He prepared a shot.

She rolled up her sleeve.

The needle pricked, then stung.

The doctor disposed of the needle in a plastic container, tucked it and the syringe in a black satchel then pulled out a bottle of pills.

"These should do the trick—one tablet three times a day with food."

"Thanks, Stan." Mitch shook the man's hand. "Anything else?"

"Lots of rest and keep an eye on that leg. If any red streaking or discharge develops, call me."

"Will do." Mitch ushered him out, then turned back to her. "You hungry?"

She shook her head. "I need to go to the bathroom."

"I'll help you, and then I'll have Mom warm up some soup for you." Mitch supported her weight as she stood.

Each step was heavy, unbalanced. "But I'm not hungry."

"You haven't eaten since we left the hospital." He walked her into the bathroom. "We need to get your strength back up, and you have to take your medicine with food. Maybe a little broth."

"Can I have some privacy now?"

"I don't want you to pass out again. Or fall."

"Well, you can't stay in here."

"Mom?"

"No. I'm feeling better now."

"No light-headedness?" He scrutinized her eyes.

"None."

Mitch left her alone.

Breathing right again, she sank to the side of the tub and covered her face with both hands. How could she possibly be all right with Mitch hovering? Reminding her of how much she loved him.

\* \* \*

Her chest rose and fell with even breaths. The red swelling around her wound had eased. Every once in a while, Mitch gently touched her cheek to make sure the fever hadn't returned.

A soft knock sounded on the door.

Mitch hurried to open it.

"How is she?" Tara leaned against the door frame.

"Resting. No fever."

"You've been here for two days and nights, Mitch."

"I know this isn't the family time you imagined."

"That's not what I'm worried about." She crossed her arms over her chest. "You must be exhausted. Want me to sit with her awhile?"

"I'm fine." He sank into the recliner. "This chair actually sleeps pretty good."

"Won't you at least come down and have supper with us tonight? Cody arrives this evening and Dad'll be here in the morning."

"We'll see."

"You need to marry her, you know."

Yes, he did. But he'd tried that once and Caitlyn had refused.

"The forensics position could fix everything. Have you even told her about it?"

"No. I'm not sure I'll get it. And you won't tell her, either."

Tara rolled her eyes and turned away.

Perched on the side of her bed, he touched her cheek. Cool.

Her eyes opened. The first time she'd awakened—without his prompting—in two days.

"Hey. How do you feel?"

"Better." She frowned. "I think. How long did I sleep?"

"Two days."

"Two days?" She pressed a hand to her mouth. "What time is it? What day is it?"

"It's almost lunchtime. Wednesday. Stan said to let you rest while your body fought off the infection."

"Did I dream it or did you keep waking me up to pour soup down me, make me take a huge pill with great potential to choke a horse and carry me to the bathroom?"

"I'm afraid it was no dream." He grinned. "But your leg looks great. I mean—" she'd always had great legs "—the infection seems to be gone."

A haunted look took root deep in her eyes. "Any breaks?"

"I wish." He shrugged. "Nothing."

Her shoulders sagged. "I'm starving."

"You are?" Excitement tinged his voice. She was on the mend. "I'll go get you some broth."

"Ugh." Her mouth twisted. "Please give me something I can chew with the potential to cover the taste of the horse pill."

"I'm on it." He headed for the door.

"Can I go down for lunch?"

"Wow." He turned to face her. "You must be feeling a lot better."

"I am. And I've inconvenienced your grandfather with an unexpected guest and never even said hello to him."

"It's no inconvenience having you here." His heart warmed. If only he could keep her near forever. "But let's take things slow. Let me bring up a tray for lunch and maybe you can come down for supper."

"All right." She nodded.

And maybe if he took things slow with her, he could keep her near. If he could figure out a way to relieve her fears. Even if he didn't get the transfer.

What must his family think of her sleeping away entire days? She'd zonked out again and hadn't made it down for supper last night.

Caitlyn smoothed her hand over the grape long-sleeved T-shirt with sparkles and spangles in darker plum shades. Her favorite colors, plus her favorite jeans with rhinestones across the back pockets.

It felt so good to wear real clothes. Her own clothes. If only she could wear her matching high-heeled boots. But they were in Aubrey and she probably needed to stick with the tennis shoes her mom had packed anyway.

A tap at her door.

"Come in." She took a deep breath.

The door swung open to reveal Tara. Not Mitch.

Caitlyn started breathing again. "Look at you, all grown up."

"I'd better be, since I'm getting married next week."

"That's crazy. Aren't you still sixteen?"

"Yeah. And you're still eighteen. How are you feeling?"

"Old." Caitlyn plopped on the bed. "And stuck in a time warp. It's like the past ten years never happened."

"That's because—" Tara laughed "—you're still madly in love with my brother and he's still madly in love with you."

Caitlyn's cheeks warmed.

"You know." Tara settled on the bed beside her. "I used to watch y'all back when the big romance was going on and hope that someday I'd find a true and lasting love like y'alls."

"I hope—" Caitlyn shook her head "—you found something a lot stronger than Mitch and I had."

"You two still love each other. It's as plain as the difference between a gray appaloosa and a dapple gray."

Caitlyn laughed. "Spoken like a girl raised on an Aubrey horse ranch."

"No changing the subject." Tara wagged a finger at her. "What happened between y'all? I thought after he finished his trooper training in Austin, he'd propose and y'all would live happily ever after. All of a sudden, it was over. Mitch wouldn't even talk about it before he moved to Garland."

Their almost happy ever after still haunted her. She took a deep breath and closed her eyes. "He did propose. But I said no."

"Really? Why?"

"Remember the first time I met your grandfather?" Caitlyn smoothed her hand over the pale yellow, green and blue quilt stitched by Tara's grandmother.

"When he and Grandma came to Aubrey for Thanksgiving."

"Yes. And he told tale after tale of dangerous Texas Ranger assignments he'd had, culminating with his partner dying in a shoot-out. Until then, Mitch being a ranger seemed honorable and noble. After hearing your grandfather's tales…"

"You got a glimpse of the dangerous side."

Caitlyn nodded. "When Mitch got accepted as a trooper at Garland, I knew he was on the road to fulfilling his dream as a Texas Ranger. I put my fears aside and decided I'd be happy for him and fully support him. He wanted me to meet him at the Ever After Chapel that weekend and I figured he planned to propose." Her voice quivered. "I fully intended to say yes and plan our wedding."

"So what happened?" Tara touched her elbow.

"A few days before our meeting, my high school friend Ally stopped by. We giggled and planned my wedding." Her chest tightened as if it were yesterday.

"Until a police car pulled into our drive. Since her dad was a trooper, we thought it was him." She pressed a hand to her heart. "But it was her mom and another trooper." She cleared her throat. "Ally's dad had died in a shoot-out."

Tara squeezed her hand.

"I watched them grieve on our front porch." Caitlyn pressed her fingertips against her lips and shook her head.

"In that moment, I knew I couldn't do it. I couldn't put my child through that. And I couldn't be that widow."

"You were scared."

"Terrified. But for as long as I could remember, Mitch dreamed of being a Texas Ranger. I couldn't ask him to give that up."

"So you said no. Even though you loved him."

Caitlyn nodded. "I thought we could each get on with our lives."

"He needs you." Tara patted her hand. "He hasn't been the same since Dylan died."

"Dylan?"

"His partner died last year. It hit Mitch hard. He even quit going to church. I thought he might be seeing someone and he might be on the mend—"

"Ahem." Mitch cleared his throat from the doorway.

"How long have you been there?" Tara shot him a look.

"Just came upstairs." Mitch frowned. "How's this for hands off?" He held a set of crutches. "Got these from Stan. Figured you could lean on them instead of me."

Caitlyn sucked in a shaky breath and dabbed her fingertips under each eye. Seeing someone. Mitch was seeing someone.

"You okay?" Mitch's frown deepened.

"Fine. Thanks for the crutches." She had some nut wanting to take her *home,* or kill her trying, plus a hole in her calf, and she was stuck with the man she'd tried to forget for the past ten years, though he'd moved on to see someone new. What could possibly be wrong?

"Let's get you downstairs." He helped her with the crutches. "After you eat, I thought you'd probably want to call your folks."

"That sounds nice." Her vision blurred and a tear slipped down her cheek.

If she could just get through the next two weeks. Wait,

she'd already slept through three days. This was Thursday. Only a little over a week left. And maybe they'd catch Stevens before then. She could do this.

She swung the crutches forward but lost her balance.

"Careful." A firm hand clutched her arm. "Slow down, hotshot. Have you ever used crutches before?"

"No. It's harder than it looks."

A week and a half. At the most. With Mitch. And her jumbled heart turning over at every glance he shot her way. While he was seeing someone new.

Mitch gritted his teeth as Caitlyn made slow, swinging progress down the stairs with her crutches. Maybe he should have given them to her after he carried her down.

"You okay?"

"Fine."

"You can stop and catch your breath."

"She said she's fine." Tara shot him a back-off frown as she led the way to the dining room.

At least Caitlyn had mastered the crutches.

With ease, she swung her way across the hardwood but stopped at the double doors. "Hold up, Tara."

Mitch chose his words carefully. "Something wrong?"

"Just kind of feel like I'm crashing a family gathering."

"You're family." Tara patted her arm. "Or we all wanted you to be anyway."

Pink splashed Caitlyn's cheeks as Tara pushed the doors open. "Look who decided to join us."

His parents, Grandpa and Cody surrounded the oval pedestal table.

"Hey, stranger." Cody bounded to Caitlyn's side and gave her a bear hug.

"Easy." Mitch's jaw clenched. "Don't bowl her over."

"When did you get here?" Delight filled her tone.

Why couldn't seeing Mitch make her that happy?

"About seven o'clock last night. You were asleep, sleepy-head. You never were much on mornings, but some people have lives, bulls to ride, people to see."

"Just getting my beauty rest." Caitlyn playfully punched him in the shoulder.

His mouth twisted to the side. "Don't think you got enough from the looks of things."

"Jerk." She punched him harder.

"You know I'm kidding." He held his hands up in sur-render. "You look great. If Mitch hadn't filled me in, I'd have never guessed some crazy guy was after you, you'd been stabbed and just got over a nasty infection."

Mom gasped. "Cody!"

A hush silenced the room.

Caitlyn burst into giggles and patted his cheek. "You're still one of a kind."

Tension whooshed away as if blown by the wind.

"If there's a longhorn in the room everybody's ignoring, leave it to Cody, he'll shoo it to the north forty." Grandpa guffawed and slapped his knee.

As Cody took Caitlyn's crutches and helped her hobble to a chair, she didn't even snarl at him.

The easy friendship between his brother and the love of his life grated Mitch's nerves raw. He wanted to snarl.

They'd been in the same class in school and it had al-ways been that way between them. Cody could get away with saying anything to her and she'd laugh. While if Mitch popped off something outrageous, she'd have slapped him. Or cried. Cody could probably get away with carrying her up the stairs and all over the house.

"I'm sorry I've been such a lazy houseguest, Mr. War-ren." Caitlyn aimed a sheepish grin at Grandpa.

"Call me Tex. We've got too many Warrens in this house to be so formal. Gets confusing." Grandpa claimed his seat at the head of the table. "And no apology needed.

You've had a few things going on. Glad you could join us for lunch."

"Thank y'all for letting Mitch bring me here." Caitlyn scanned the faces at the table. "The last thing I wanted was to crash the wedding preparations, but Mitch gave me little choice."

"Nonsense." Tara passed the basket of rolls. "I invited you to my wedding. Instead, I get a bunking party. It'll be fun."

"We're glad to have you." Mitch's father passed the fried squash. "And you can call me Wayne now that you're all grown up."

"It's wonderful having you here." Mom glanced at Mitch. "Just like old times."

Not exactly. Caitlyn was happy to see them all, except Mitch.

The fresh air and hot sun felt good on Caitlyn's skin even as a bead of sweat trickled down her spine. Live oaks reached toward the trail on each side of them with twisted, knobby limbs.

"Oh, Cody, this was exactly what I needed. Thank you."

"No problem. Watch out for that little dip there. Don't get a crutch hung in it."

Leaves that had been stripped from the trees during the weekend downpour littered the path. The more hardy trees remained green. At least for another month or so.

The crutches chafed her underarms, but it was worth it to be outside. The wooded trail beside the ranch house opened into a clearing where a dozen palominos grazed. Two hundred yards away, a cabin sat in the distance beside a serene pond.

"Is that Mitch's cabin?"

"Yep."

"Why does he have a cabin here?"

"He and Grandpa built it last year. After Mitch's partner died."

"Does he come here much?"

"Not as often as he should." He cut in front of her, walking backward to face her. "Did we come out here to talk about Mitch?"

"Just curious."

"You've still got it bad for him." He turned back toward the path.

She let him get ahead of her a bit, then whacked her crutch across his backside.

"Ow," Cody yelped. "Hey, what did I do?"

"Let's not talk about Mitch. Tell me about you."

"I'm not the one who brought him up." Cody teased in a singsong tone.

She raised her crutch.

"Okay. Change of subject. Let's see. Still riding bulls. Traveling the circuit all over Texas."

"Anyone special?"

"Nah. I'm never in the same place long enough for anything to develop."

"Don't you ever get tired of the road?" Caitlyn pulled at her shirtsleeve, trying to get more fabric between her and the crutch. "Do you ever think of settling down, growing some roots?"

"Not so far. Guess I haven't met the right person yet."

"Sometimes when you do," she said, and sighed, "it still doesn't work out."

"Now who's talking about Mitch?"

"I didn't say a word about him."

"You didn't have to."

"You still tease me like you did when we were teenagers? Will you never grow up?"

"Not if I don't have to. Just call me Peter Pan." He turned to face her again, walking backward. "And you're so much fun to tease. Your face turns about a dozen different shades."

"Caitlyn!" Mitch's call echoed through the clearing.

She closed her eyes.

"Busted," Cody whispered.

"What do you think you're doing?" Mitch sprinted up beside her and took hold of her arm.

# Chapter 6

"I *was* having a pleasant walk in the woods." Caitlyn jerked free. "What does it look like I'm doing?"

"It was my idea." Cody sucked in an overly dramatic deep breath. "I thought she needed some fresh air. Does a body good."

"What part of protective custody do you not understand?"

Caitlyn rolled her eyes. "My attacker is in Fort Worth."

"We don't know that. And you're supposed to be resting your leg."

"You didn't tell me that." Cody frowned at her.

"I was dying to get out of the house." She shrugged. "We took extreme precautions to make sure we weren't followed. I thought I was safe."

"Listen to me, Caitlyn." Mitch settled his hands gently on her shoulders. His intense green gaze snagged hers. And wouldn't let go. "I'll do everything in my power to keep you safe. Once we get this guy in custody, you can get all the fresh air you want. But until then, we can't be too careful. I won't let him hurt you again."

"Mitch is right. I wasn't thinking. Let's head back." Cody's words came from far away as she drowned in Mitch's eyes. She saw caring there, but also fear for her safety.

"I'm tired anyway." She turned toward the house, each swing of her crutches hurried and frantic. To get away from Mitch. Her blistered underarms stung. They shouldn't have gone so far.

"Caitlyn, be careful." Mitch reached for her. "Let me help you."

"Hey, hold up. I've got an idea." Cody took her crutches and handed them to Mitch.

"What are you doing?"

"This." Cody scooped her over his shoulder caveman style and headed for the house.

"You're insane." She laughed.

Cody always had the ability to make her laugh—while Mitch had the ability to make her cry.

From the doorway of the huge family room, Mitch supervised as Cody and Tara helped Caitlyn settle in the large window seat. Not even the sectional sofa with recliners at each end and the oversize coffee table could make this room small.

"There. See, you still get sunshine." Cody caught his eye. "That is, if Mitch approves?"

"The alarm on the gate and house are both activated."

Caitlyn rolled her eyes.

"Let's play a game. Or do a puzzle." Tara opened the closet and scanned the family game collection stacked neatly on the shelves. "We could play Pictionary."

"Me and Tara against Mitch and Caitlyn." Cody rubbed his hands together. "Like old times."

"Feel like getting beat, huh?" Mitch strode into the room. Caitlyn and he had always won that game. He had artistic ability while she had none. But the timer in the game didn't allow for artistry and he'd always known what she was trying to draw as if they were on the same wavelength. When it came to games, anyway. He scooted the game table in front of Caitlyn.

"Y'all don't have to play games and babysit me."

"We love games." Tara set the game on the table and grabbed two chairs. "And we're never all together like this anymore. Mom, Grandpa—want to play?"

"Nah, you young folks go ahead. I'll just sit here and laugh at you." Grandpa winked at Caitlyn.

Mom's crochet needle looped through the yarn at a quick pace, leaving an intricate pattern in its wake. "I've got a dozen lap blankets left to finish for the nursing home by Christmas."

"I could help you. I remember everything you taught me." Caitlyn obviously wasn't interested in partnership with him. In any capacity.

"That would be great. But you play your game, since y'all have even teams. You can help me crochet later."

Caitlyn's shoulders slumped as Mitch took a seat beside her. "Sure you're comfy?"

"I was." Her words came under her breath as if she didn't mean to say them at all.

But Mitch heard. She was comfy. Until he got there. "Y'all go first. You might need a head start."

"We're gonna mop the floor with you." Cody rolled his eyes and drew a card.

As Caitlyn set the hourglass timer, Cody started drawing. An oblong circle took shape.

"A bean?" Tara guessed.

Cody shook his head.

"A pea?"

With a theatrical sigh, Cody jabbed his pencil against what he'd drawn.

"You gotta give me more than that." Tara laughed. "It looks like a bean or a pea. Corn?"

Every guess Tara made caused Cody to shake his head with increasing force and jab the paper.

Mitch watched the last of the sand trickle through the hourglass. "Time's up."

"No fair. He can't draw worth a flip." Tara grinned.

"It's a banana. Don't you know a banana when you see one?"

"That's one sad-looking banana." Caitlyn laughed.

"Well, we can't all be an artist like Mitch."

"The game doesn't allow time for artistry." Mitch handed Caitlyn their sketch pad. "Here, I'll let Caitlyn draw first."

"Ready." Tara turned the timer over. "Go."

As Caitlyn drew, Mitch huddled close, her hair brushing against his ear. Her perfume dizzied his brain. A misshapen bird took form on the paper with stick legs and talons, but he didn't want to give up her closeness, and so he let half the sand drain. "A bird."

She nodded, then drew a triangle on the bird's head.

A little more sand trickled through as he glanced at the timer. "A cardinal. A blue jay."

"Blue jay." She moved away from him.

"No fair." Cody harrumphed. "That was easy."

"Not really." Tara chuckled. "That bird kind of looks like a fly."

"Really?" Caitlyn smirked. "Let me see your blue jay."

Mitch spent the afternoon soundly beating his brother and sister, interpreting Caitlyn's stick figures and kitten-resembling lions and sparing the details and perfection in his own sketching while watching her tension fade away. And reveling in her nearness.

\* \* \*

The soft yarn and mindless repetitive movement of her crochet hook relaxed Caitlyn. She wasn't as fast as Mitch's mom, but she kept a pretty good pace. "It's really nice to make lap blankets for the nursing-home patients."

"Our church has been doing it for several years. Each year, we pick a different nursing home somewhere in Texas, find out how many patients they have and send blankets. I like to think each stitch is crocheted with love and, hopefully, it makes the patients feel not forgotten."

Caitlyn glanced toward Mitch. His gaze was still on her. Hers flitted back to her work.

He'd stared at her all day. If he was seeing someone new, why wouldn't he stop staring at her?

Gathered in the family room, the scents of the cedar walls and the sectional sofa's rich, taupe leather permeated the room. Tara curled up in the window seat reading while Cody played Angry Birds and Grandpa watched *Wheel of Fortune.*

Mitch stared at Caitlyn.

Her shoulders tensed, and she stretched them.

Three of Lyla's quilts softened the room—one on the back of each couch section and one hanging on the wall. Caitlyn had once looked forward to receiving one of Mitch's grandmother's quilts as a wedding gift.

"You can take a break if you need to." Audra gently stilled Caitlyn's hands.

"No, I'm fine." It wasn't crocheting binding up her muscles.

"I wish you could go shopping with us tomorrow." Tara set her novel down.

"With all the suitcases you brought, you're going shopping?" Mitch rubbed the back of his neck. "My shoulders haven't recovered from your trousseau thingy yet."

Caitlyn smiled. But she didn't want to think about his shoulders.

"I still need a few things for the house. Towels, sheets, dishes—that sort of thing."

"After four wedding showers?" Cody never looked up from his Kindle Fire.

"It takes a lot of stuff to set up a house." Tara rolled her eyes. "Not all of us aspire to live out of a truck and motels."

"Don't knock it until you try it."

"No, thanks." Tara scrunched her nose. "What is it with men? Mitch's apartment is barely furnished and last time we were there, he didn't even have any dishes."

"Paper doesn't require washing. And I don't really live there—I just sleep there. But look at my cabin."

So where did he live? At his new girlfriend's place? At least he didn't sleep there. That he admitted, anyway.

"You win on that one." Tara rolled her eyes. "Caitlyn, you have to get Mitch to show you his cabin. It's not very female friendly, but it has a certain charm. It's like walking through Bass Pro."

"I imagine Caitlyn's never been to Bass Pro." Cody laughed. "Not her style."

"It's not on my bucket list." Caitlyn dropped a loop and picked it back up.

"That's where we need to take Tara for her dishes, towels and sheets." Cody framed the air with his hands. "I can see it now. Jared and Tara's Bass Pro Ranch."

"No way."

Caitlyn smiled at the gentle teasing. She loved this family. Content to be together—each occupied with their hobbies or interests. Except for Mitch. If only he'd find something to do other than stare at her.

And this was only week one of her stay. Time stretched before her with Tara's wedding a week from tomorrow. How would she deal with a whole second week of his proximity?

\* \* \*

Why did Cody get to help Caitlyn hop up the stairs for the evening? Why couldn't Mitch have the easy camaraderie with her that his brother had?

Being so close to her was paradise. Only with two very large shadows. Number one—she was in danger. Number two—she didn't want to be close to him.

Number one he could do something about. He pulled up his phone's address book and punched a number.

"Remington Ranch."

"Quinn, it's Mitch Warren. I've got a proposition for you."

"About Trent's dad?"

"I promise we'll keep Trent safe."

"What do you want Trent to do?"

"The quickest way to land a fish is to use the right bait."

"Trent?" Quinn's tone turned gruff. "No. I won't endanger the boy. He's been through enough—thanks to his so-called father."

"Just hear me out. We could clear your ranch and replace your employees with rangers. Plus extras. I know every nook and cranny of the place. We'd have it crawling with law enforcement."

Silence ticked several seconds away.

Quinn sighed. "Couldn't you use a decoy instead of Trent?"

"Stevens knows his son. And he may be crazy, but he's not stupid." Yes, he'd had problems recognizing his wife. But from the picture Mitch had seen, that was understandable.

"On one condition."

"I'm listening."

"My family leaves, my employees leave but I'm staying."

From what Mitch knew of Quinn, he'd expected it. "Done."

"And Trent can't miss any school. This will have to go down over the weekend."

"I'll contact Timmons at headquarters and he'll be in contact."

"You won't be involved?"

He'd like to be. He'd like to take Stevens in himself. And beat him to a pulp in transport. "I'm protecting the victim."

"Just see that you protect Trent. And my family."

"You have nothing to worry about. You have my word." Mitch ended the call.

"You gonna tell her what's going on?" Grandpa turned a piece of his jigsaw puzzle every which way trying to make it fit.

"No. Not until it's over."

If the operation went well, Stevens's reign of terror would be over. Caitlyn would walk out of Mitch's life. Again.

But at least she'd be safe. And in the meantime, he'd spend every possible moment with her.

Saturday morning, Jared arrived and everyone prepared for lunch in Medina and the shopping trip in San Antonio. Except Mitch. And Caitlyn.

Even Grandpa was going. Mitch knew Grandpa couldn't care less about shopping, but he took every opportunity to spend time with his family.

Discontent showed in every tight muscle that made up Caitlyn's slim form and every line on her face. She sat by Grandpa, staring at a jigsaw puzzle. With her leg healing nicely, her lone crutch leaned against the arm of the couch.

A vibration startled Mitch. He dug his phone out of his pocket.

Headquarters. His heart jolted. "Warren here."

Caitlyn's gaze caught his.

"Stevens was at his brother's in Fort Worth about thirty

minutes ago." Timmons's tone sounded grave. "He had a broken bone in his wrist. His brother pretended to go for meds and called police, but Stevens bolted before they got there."

Mitch massaged the bridge of his nose. "Keep me updated."

"Did something happen?" Caitlyn's voice trembled.

"Stevens was in Fort Worth about thirty minutes ago. But he got away."

"That means he doesn't know where I am?" Her mouth formed a small O. "But Natalie's helping with the store."

"He wasn't anywhere near your store. Besides, she's safe. You hired a new clerk at each store before you left on business."

"No, I didn't." She frowned.

"An undercover ranger."

"Oh." She closed her eyes. "Thank you."

"This calls for celebration, I think." Grandpa slid a piece of the puzzle in place.

"We didn't get him." Mitch frowned.

"No. But we know he's five hours away. I think Caitlyn's got ranch fever. This means she could join our outing today."

Her eyes lit up. "Could I?"

*No* hovered on Mitch's tongue. What if Stevens's brother was providing a cover so Stevens could slip away to Medina? No. If he knew where Caitlyn was, he'd have shown up by now.

"Come on, son. Lighten up. Even if anything were to go wrong—and it won't—you'd be right there to keep her safe."

Mitch sighed. "You sure your leg's up for it?"

"If I get tired, I promise I'll sit down."

"When we intrepid shoppers head for San Antonio, y'all

could come back here and tour the ranch." Grandpa picked up another puzzle piece.

"Fort Worth is five hours from here." Mitch shrugged. "We'll stay gone three hours—max—to be on the safe side."

"Agreed." She stood and picked up her crutches. "Let me go upstairs a minute."

"Take your time. Mom and Tara aren't ready yet. Need help with the stairs?"

"I'm good." She slid the crutches under her arms. "And, Mitch—thanks."

Finally, he'd done something right with her. "I'm glad you're getting a break."

Slowly, she climbed the stairs.

Wonderful scents of cinnamon and apple emanated from the Apple Store. The shelves burst with syrups, breads and pancake mixes, plus every possible apple-based jam, jelly and preserve. Caitlyn narrowed her purchases to apple-pumpkin bread, apple-peach-cobbler jam and apple butter.

After the ladies had paid for their goodies, they ordered lunch and sat at a red picnic table in the pavilion-type dining area behind the store.

"How is it?" Audra sipped her tea.

Caitlyn dabbed her mouth with a napkin. "I love a good cheeseburger."

"Wait till you taste the bread and jellies." Tara rolled her eyes. "To die for." She gasped as she realized her word choice.

"Who's up for apple pie and ice cream?" Mitch stood.

"Me." All voices joined in unison.

Cody and Jared went along to help with the orders.

"Are you sure you won't go shopping with us, Caitlyn?" Tara asked. "It'll be so much fun."

"To be honest, I'm not sure my leg is up to it yet."

"Oh, I forgot. But you'll be all healed soon and this confinement thing won't last forever. Maybe next week. And in the meantime, Mitch can show you around the ranch." Tara's enthusiasm was almost contagious. "You haven't even seen the river and you can tour the apple orchard here. Next month they open the pumpkin patch and all the schools have field trips. I got to volunteer one year. So much fun."

"Surely I'll be home before October."

"And the river might be a bit cool this time of year." Grandpa chuckled.

"Not for fishing. Jared and I plan to go tomorrow."

"A week before your wedding and you want to go fishing. You're making your grandpa proud."

The men returned, each carrying two bowls. Mitch set one in front of Caitlyn and one in front of Grandpa, then went back to get his own.

The double-crust pie was the perfect mixture of gooey and flaky sweetness. The apple ice cream melted in her mouth.

"We were just talking, Mitch. You need to take Caitlyn to the river today." Tara licked her spoon clean. "She'd love it, and you have to take her to your cabin."

Caitlyn's heart sped up. "I'd just as soon go back to the house."

"But you never know when you'll get another chance to escape." Tara sounded so natural, as if she had no ulterior motives. "You should take advantage of it."

"We could all tour together." She hoped Tara heard the plea in her tone.

"By the time Tara buys out all the stores, it'll be too dark." Cody grinned. "I'm up for skipping the shopping trip and touring the ranch."

"No." Tara elbowed him. "You have work to do."

"I do?"

"Something about rodeo research."

"Oh, that." Cody cleared his throat. "I've got rodeo research to do."

"Rodeo research?" Caitlyn eyes narrowed.

"I need to check the standings. Me and another rider are neck and neck for the lead."

Like that took hours. Mitch's entire family was conspiring to get her alone with him.

And Caitlyn didn't want alone time with Mitch. Truth be told—she did. But she didn't want to want alone time with Mitch. Why did he always confuse her so badly?

Mitch strolled toward Grandpa's ranch house. The soon-to-be-married couple had barely taken their eyes off each other during lunch. Seeing his sister so happy and loved warmed his heart. If only he could have the woman he loved.

But a drover could drive a longhorn or two through the gap Caitlyn carefully kept between her and Mitch.

At least they were alone, with Cody on his research mission.

His family. Mitch held back a grin. Always eager to help him out, but not always subtle about it.

"How about we tour the ranch on horseback?" He narrowed the gap.

Her eyes lit up, but her pace increased. "Maybe I should call it a day."

"Come on." Mitch checked his watch. "You've got another hour and a half before Cinderella's carriage turns into a pumpkin. This might be the last time you get out of the house for a while."

"I don't have any boots." Her shoulders slumped.

"Tara and Mom do. What size do you wear?"

"Seven."

"I'll check. They're not your usual style—less sparkle—

but they'll work if they fit. Have a seat on the porch and I'll check."

Caitlyn climbed the steps and settled on the wagon-wheel bench.

Maybe with his whole family behind him, he could finagle time with her and inch his way back into her heart.

Caitlyn's rhinestone-studded jeans and blouse didn't go with Tara's plain brown boots. But Mitch matched her. He'd changed into riding clothes—a teal Western shirt that blended with her aqua blingy blouse.

They'd always done that. Shown up wearing similar colors with no preplanning. Caitlyn dreaded the moment his family saw them, well aware Tara would comment on their compatibility. If only compatibility could be based on blending colors instead of life-and-death choices.

Concentrate on the scenery instead of the man on horse-back at her side. The trail behind the ranch led to a narrow crossing at the river. The water rippled over white river rocks, and huge, feathery-leaved cypress trees stretched their clawlike roots into the water.

Mitch turned his horse toward the cabin path. Reluctantly, Caitlyn followed.

"Your family hasn't changed a bit." Caitlyn tried to relax, letting her body move in rhythm with the palomino. The horse's buttery coat and creamy mane glistened in the sunlight.

"They've always loved you." Mitch kept his matching horse in step with hers. "Good thing you don't get motion sickness on horseback."

"No. Just cars, buses and escalators. So far. Natalie's tried to get me on a plane, but she hasn't won yet."

"How's Natalie? I heard she married Lane Grey." Disbelief tinged his voice.

"Much better. She told me about running into you in a bar last spring." But not until recently.

"For the record, I was working a case."

"Duh. Mr. Straight-and-Narrow. Thanks for trying to help her. She's doing great now."

"I gotta tell you, I worried about her after seeing her in that bar."

"She and Lane are both Christians now and it turns out they've been in love since high school." Sounds familiar. Where Caitlyn's heart was concerned, anyway. A little ache throbbed to life in her chest. "She gets to see her daughter just about any time she wants, and they're doing great."

"She has a daughter?"

"Back in her wild days, she got pregnant and signed custody over to the father. But now that she's settled down, he lets Nat see Hannah."

"I'm glad it worked out well."

"Hannah is a darling." Caitlyn patted her horse. "Her dad is a bull rider and, at first, he wouldn't let us see Hannah. I guess he was afraid we'd try to take her away. But eventually he relented and I bonded with my niece."

"You always wanted kids."

Her stomach knotted. Mitch's kids. "Hannah's part of the reason I took the rodeo-queen gig. I used to keep her on Friday or Saturday nights—sometimes both. But since Nat's back in the picture, I'm not needed as much and Hannah left a big hole in my weekends." Sadness rang clear in her tone. Did he hear it?

"I'm sure she still needs you. And maybe someday you'll have kids of your own." He chuckled. "But the rodeo-queen gig might not be conducive to motherhood, since it ties up your date nights."

Why did her imagined date nights include him, and why did her imagined child look like him? A lump formed in her throat.

"So did you have to compete for your title?"

"Sort of. I applied, provided the right clothing and showed them I could ride well, hold a flag upright and display poise. I did run barrels to show I could still compete. I think I'm the oldest queen they've ever hired."

"Yep, getting downright long in the tooth." Mitch shot her a heart-melting grin.

"I feel that way when I see the backup queens—still in their teens." Caitlyn slapped her reins, urging her horse to a trot. They emerged in the clearing with the cabin in the distance.

"After the cabin, we'll have to go back." Mitch's horse surged up beside her and he checked his watch.

The horses' canter ate up the clearing and they slowed as they neared the cabin.

"How often do you come here?"

"Not as much as Grandpa thinks I need to. He wanted me to have a place to get away from…things."

Why did he have to bring up his job? She slid off her horse.

Mitch waited as she climbed the porch steps, then followed and slid a key in the lock.

Cedar siding filled her senses. No graying on the log exterior, just the rich rust-colored wood streaked with yellow tones. "How do you keep it so vibrant?"

"I have it treated twice a year." He opened the door and ushered her inside.

Inside, the walls were log, as well. The living room sofa boasted a woodsy scene with deer leaping, a matching recliner and camouflage curtain toppers. The coffee table was built from logs and covered with gun and truck magazines. A rug bearing the image of a large buck complemented the rustic surroundings. An enormous TV, surrounded by dead animal heads, took up most of one wall.

"You hunt now?"

"No. It's Grandpa's collection. Grandma never liked them, so they've been in storage. He thought they fit better here than at the ranch."

"I was sorry to hear about her illness. She was a sweet lady."

"The best." His gaze went to a built-in corner shelf filled with family photos. A picture of his grandparents—their smiles genuine, captured for eternity.

"Let me show you around." He ushered her to the kitchen.

Saltshakers shaped like tree stumps with an antler thrown in for good measure sat on the cedar-log table. Plates featuring a buck in the middle and rimmed with camouflage lined open cedar shelves grooved to hold them in place.

"I feel way too feminine to be here." Her heart skittered in fine female form. Alone with Mitch in his most private getaway.

"You're welcome anytime." Mitch grinned and opened a drawer. "Check out the silverware I got the last time I was here."

Even the silverware had a buck head at the base.

"You have to see my bathroom. I may have gotten carried away. It's through the bedroom." Mitch led her back through the living room and gestured her to a doorway.

Through his bedroom.

Caitlyn's stomach turned.

Would there be traces of the new woman in his life there? A lingering perfume scent? Pictures? Feminine touches?

She traipsed through his bedroom to find a brown suede-look comforter with a Texas-lone-star border. Fishing rods decorated the walls along with several stuffed fish. She scanned the rustic cedar dresser. No pictures. None on the log nightstand, either. If the new woman in his life had invaded his heart, at least she hadn't invaded this part of his life.

"Check it out." Mitch stopped in the bathroom doorway.

Deer-antler toilet paper, towel and toothbrush holders with the obligatory camouflage shower curtain and towels.

"It looks almost dangerous. A person could get gored."

Mitch laughed. "I've had fun with it. All my friends love it. They're all married, so they could never get away with any of this. Who knows, I might have to get rid of it one day." His gaze caught hers.

Her throat closed up. She bolted blindly back toward the living room.

"Caitlyn?"

"We'd better get back."

"Right." His hands settled gently on her shoulders. "Listen, I'm certain you're safe. I don't want you to be scared, but I won't take any chances."

Thank goodness he thought her jumpiness came from fear of her stalker instead of fear of someday reading his engagement announcement in the paper.

"We should get this guy soon."

Then she could go home. Leave Mitch behind. And he could resume his life with his someone new.

So why could she so easily imagine living here? With Mitch, minus a few dead things. Why did he have to be so noble? So good? Make her feel so safe?

He opened the door and she stepped ahead of him. Eyes burning, she blinked away the threatening moisture.

A blast went off. She jumped.

A scream escaped her as Mitch tackled her and they both went rolling back inside the cabin.

## *Chapter* 7

Mitch clamped his hand over Caitlyn's mouth and kicked the door shut. With his body splayed over hers, his gun drawn, he listened. Nothing.

"Quiet. Don't move," he whispered, and rolled off her.

Huge sapphire eyes stared up at him.

He gently touched her cheek, then turned the coffee table over to its side and pulled it in front of her for a makeshift barricade. He'd let his guard down and Caitlyn could have been shot. But he'd have to kick himself later. Mitch crawled across to the window.

No movement in the clearing except the horses, their ears alert, hides flinching.

Another blast. In the distance.

Caitlyn yelped.

"Relax." His breathing eased. "It's coming from far away. Sorry. I didn't realize that at the first shot, I just reacted. It's probably a hunter over on the next ranch. Deer season opens soon."

No response.

Mitch turned to face her.

Curled in a tight ball behind his coffee table, silent sobs racked her entire body.

"Oh, Caitlyn. I'm sorry I scared you. You're safe." He gathered her in his arms.

With her face pressed into his chest, her sobs found sound.

And turned him inside out. "You're safe with me. I'll never, ever let anything happen to you."

Through all her turmoil, she'd been so tough. But now the emotion she'd kept in check had caught up with her.

He held her tight, wishing he could tell her how much he loved her. How much he wanted to keep her safe. For the rest of her life.

The next morning, Caitlyn stayed in her bed, listening to everyone's movements. The stirring quieted and she heard voices outside, then vehicles leaving.

Just her and Mitch. Alone in the house. She rolled over with her back to the bedroom door. If she stayed here, she'd be safe from Stuart Stevens. And safe from Mitch.

And if he wasn't close to her, he couldn't take a bullet for her. She hadn't really thought about it until yesterday—keeping her safe put him in danger.

Her eyes felt swollen and her lids heavy. She'd barely slept last night and when she had, she'd relived her attack in her dreams.

A gentle tap on her door. "Caitlyn."

She didn't answer. Held her breath.

"I know you couldn't have slept through all the chaos. You hungry?"

Maybe if she answered, he'd go away. "I'm fine."

"Can I come in?"

"I don't need anything."

"Can I come in?"

She sighed and pulled the covers tighter. "Yes."

The door opened. His footfalls echoed across the hardwood. His legs interrupted her line of vision.

"I know you're not used to gunshots, being taken down and stalkers. But I won't let you stay holed up in your room and be a hermit."

"That's not what I'm doing. I'm tired." *Worn-out from being exposed to you.*

"I imagine you didn't sleep much last night. Want me to get Stan to give you something?"

"No. I'm fine."

"Well, here are your choices. Either you stay here and I'll take up residence in the recliner again. Or you come downstairs, eat some breakfast and we'll watch a movie or something. Grandpa has that Hallmark Channel you always liked."

Watch a love story with Mitch? No way. "I'll come down, but no tearjerkers. Maybe we can find some good preaching to watch."

He drooped a little.

Maybe preaching was what Mitch needed. "I've missed church two Sundays and Wednesday now. I haven't missed that much church since I had the flu a few years ago."

"Fine. I'll be downstairs."

Maybe she could help him remember he needed God. Before he took a bullet for her. Or someone else.

Two sermons later, Mitch was stiffer than she'd ever seen him. His family had returned and eaten lunch, then scattered to take advantage of the lovely weather. At least Grandpa had come inside, so they weren't alone anymore.

The *Mission: Impossible* theme played and Mitch dug his phone out of his pocket. "Uh, Grandpa, I need to take this in the kitchen. Can you keep an eye on things?"

"Caitlyn and I will be fine." Grandpa patted the seat beside him at the game table. "Maybe she can find this piece I've been pulling my whiskers out over."

The music was loud, insistent.

"If anyone comes to the door—"

"I know, I know." Grandpa waved a dismissive hand. "Don't answer it unless I know 'em, and Caitlyn needs to make herself scarce."

Mitch turned toward the kitchen.

"You two need to get married, you know." Grandpa tried to fit a piece in the puzzle.

Caitlyn gasped.

"You still love each other, I can see it."

If she'd known what to say, her vocal cords surely wouldn't have responded.

"I suspect you broke his heart because the job scared you." He grinned as the piece slid in and he glanced up at her.

"How did you know that?"

"Been there, done that. I saw the same fear in Lyla's eyes for forty years."

She stared at the puzzle as if her life depended on finding the next piece.

"Broke your heart, too, I 'magine."

"We've moved on." At least, Mitch had.

"Crying shame when folks who should be together move on." Grandpa slid another piece into place. "Lyla worried about me our entire marriage. Worried I'd get shot, or knifed, or die in a car chase. I retired a Texas Ranger with nary a gunshot wound or even a broken bone." His voice broke. "Lyla never worried about cancer. She was gone at sixty-five. I've lived without her eight years now and I'm still kicking pretty good. Except in the broken-heart area."

"I'm sorry. I always loved her."

"Point is. She worried about me and she's gone. I'm

not. Just because someone is a Texas Ranger doesn't mean they'll die young. If something were to happen to Mitch—God willing, it won't—but if it were, don't you think you'd be heartbroken whether y'all were together or not?"

Mitch stepped into the room, his face unreadable.

"Something's happened?" Her voice quivered.

"They got him."

"He's in jail?" She let out a whoop.

"He shot himself." Mitch shook his head. "He's dead."

Her heart stilled. Emotions washed over her—relief the ordeal was over, guilt that she felt relieved over a death, yearning to stay close to Mitch. Her vision blurred and she pressed a shaky hand to her mouth.

"It's over." Mitch knelt beside her and pulled her into his arms.

And in spite of everything, this was right where she wanted to be. With Mitch.

A blast fired in the distance. Mitch's arms tensed—tightened around her.

"Relax, son. It's Langston next door." Grandpa peered out the curtains. "Your trouble's over."

But the distant shot served as a reminder of why she couldn't be with him. Despite her feelings, his grandfather's words, her heart—she couldn't be that widow. She just couldn't.


"But you can't leave before the wedding," Tara wailed, as if Caitlyn's departure was the end of the world.

"You weren't planning on me being here anyway." Caitlyn folded her blouse and stuffed it in her suitcase.

"No, but then once you ended up here, I did. Please, Caitlyn, you have to stay. Just until the wedding's over."

"I can't. I have two businesses and my position as rodeo queen. And I'm not in danger anymore." Her words caught.

*My attacker killed himself and Mitch is seeing someone.*
"There's no reason for me to stay."

"I'm getting married. What more reason do you need?
And it's only a few more days."

"Oh, Tara, I'd love to stay, but—"

"I originally wanted to ask you to be one of my bridesmaids."

"You did?" Caitlyn's hands stilled in her folding.

"But I didn't want you to be uncomfortable—because
of Mitch. So I sent the invitation. If you'd RSVP'd that you
were coming, I planned to ask you."

"But since I declined, you didn't. Why me? We haven't
seen each other in ten years."

"I always wished I had a sister. You were the closest
thing I ever had."

Caitlyn squelched a sigh. "If you add me to the wedding, won't that make your wedding party uneven? Jared
will have fewer groomsmen."

"He had a cousin on standby." Tara shrugged. "In case
you agreed."

"That leaves a slight dress and tux problem?"

"Once you got here, I ordered those, too. Just in case. I
guessed you wear an eight."

"Good guesser. And when were you planning to let me
in on this plan?"

"I've been praying they'd get the nut who has made your
life miserable so Mitch would let you go to the fitting and
to my outdoor wedding."

How could she let Tara down? Caitlyn inwardly sagged
at what she was about to do. "I'll check with my sister, my
store manager and my boss at the rodeo. If everything is
okay at home, I'll stay."

Tara let out a whoop. "This is awesome!"

"I still have to check on things."

But there was no cautioning Tara as she chattered about the wedding.

A knock sounded at the door. Tara danced over and swung it open.

Mitch.

"What's going on in here? It sounds like one of Tara's middle-school sleepovers."

"Caitlyn's staying for the wedding. She's going to be a bridesmaid like I originally planned."

A smile lit Mitch's eyes as his gaze met hers. "I was coming to ask if you were ready to head out."

"I have to check on my stores and my job." She lifted one shoulder. "But Tara apparently didn't hear me when I mentioned that."

"I don't think she's heard anything since Jared popped the question." Mitch playfully knocked on Tara's head.

"Have to."

His gaze swung back to Caitlyn. "Glad you're feeling better. And staying. Maybe you can have some fun now instead of being cooped up here."

"Ooh, Caitlyn, you can go to church with us tonight. And Mitch, you, too." Tara jabbed a finger at him. "Don't even try to get out of it."

Mitch looked squeamish.

*Please convince him to go, Lord. Not so I can be near him, but for his sake.*

But if she didn't know better, she'd think Tara was trying to get them back together. Did Tara not like the new woman in his life? Or could she not let go of the past?

Just like Caitlyn.

Why had she agreed to stay? Her only hope now was that the store needed her.

Caitlyn was staying—the best news Mitch had heard since learning Stevens was no longer a threat. To anyone.

Now if he could get through this church service Tara had forced on him. She'd even arranged for him to sit next to Caitlyn. His sister—pure of heart with the best of intentions—but about as subtle as a longhorn in a china shop.

Multicolored prisms burst through the stained glass windows. Old-fashioned pews held well-used hymnals in the wooden racks. Musty pages—smells from his childhood. Caitlyn's posture remained stiff. She'd put as much space between them on the pew as she could manage—a good two inches of dark green fabric between him and her frothy red dress. Obviously wishing she was anywhere other than sitting with him.

It surprised him she'd agreed to stay for another week. But then, Tara could be very persuasive.

"Turn to Romans 8:38–39," the pastor's voice boomed, and the swishing of pages echoed throughout the church. "'For I am persuaded, that neither death, nor life, nor angels, nor principalities, nor powers, nor things present, nor things to come, nor height, nor depth, nor any other creature, shall be able to separate us from the love of God, which is in Christ Jesus our Lord.'"

Not even questioning God's timing.

After Dylan died, he'd questioned God, stopped praying, stopped going to church. He'd crawled inside himself—wishing he'd been the one to die instead.

Pushing aside the fact that God was still in control. He'd forgotten to trust that God had called Dylan home. The timing fit into God's grand plan. Not Mitch's.

*Forgive me.*

He'd never understand why. Not until he got to Glory. But he had to remember—it was God's show to run. Not his.

Snippets of the rest of the sermon pierced his thoughts and heart. When the altar-call song began, he stood and hurried to the front. Legs shaking, mind blank, he knelt. God knew all that lay heavy on his heart. Movement to his right. His dad knelt by his side.

*God, take all of it. My guilt over Dylan's death, the inadequacy I feel when I fail to protect and someone dies, my relationship with Caitlyn. I can't handle it. But I know You can.*

He stood and his dad did, too. A few yards away, Caitlyn knelt at the altar. Alone.

*Go to her.*

But before he could take a step, she stood. Eyes cast down, she returned to her seat.

Despite all Tara's attempts to get Caitlyn to go shopping, she wasn't sure her leg was up to it. She sat in the window seat, pretending to read a business magazine. Why, why, why had she agreed to stay? If only she could call a cab and sneak home.

Mitch lurked nearby, watching some home-improvement show. She should have stayed in her room. Grandpa had tried to interest her in his puzzle, but she couldn't concentrate.

Movement out of the corner of her eye. Mitch. Headed in her direction.

"You okay?" He sat down on the other end of the window seat.

"Fine." She forced her gaze in his direction to find bare feet and jeans. A deadly combination for her fluttering heart.

"You're so quiet."

"Just reading."

"I can tell." He reached for the magazine, took it from her and turned it right side up.

Her face heated. "Guess I'm distracted."

"Let's go for a walk."

"I'd rather stay here."

"Caitlyn, you're safe." He took her hand.

But she pulled free. Not safe from him. "I'll stay and help Grandpa."

"Young lady, you're much too young and vibrant to sit around with an old man doing puzzles." Grandpa shooed her away. "Now git."

Mitch reclaimed her hand and gently pulled her up from the seat.

She tugged out of his grasp but followed him to the door. He put his jacket on, then helped her shrug into her coat.

Outside, stillness surrounded them except for traffic whirring in the distance, horses whinnying and birds twittering overhead.

A sparrow skittered out of a bush. Caitlyn jumped.

"You're safe." Mitch pulled her close. "Say it."

"I'm safe." Like an idiot huddled in his arms repeating a mantra that could never work. Her heart would never be safe with Mitch around.

"Just stay close."

With pleasure. With his arm around her shoulder, hers around his waist, huddled close, they walked.

After a while, she relaxed. More content than she had been in ten years. If only he hadn't moved on.

How would his someone new feel about him being sidled up to his someone old? She put some space between them.

"Hey, where'd you go?" He tried to pull her close again, but she sidestepped him.

"Tara told me…" she bit her lip "…you're seeing someone new. How would she feel about…us being close to each other?"

## Chapter 8

"I'm not seeing anyone." Mitch frowned.

Caitlyn replayed Tara's words. *I thought he was seeing someone new...* Mitch had walked in then and they'd never finished the conversation.

"I have a really good friend, but that's all she is—kind of like you and Cody. Tara thought it might grow into more, but it won't. I've told my well-intentioned sister that dozens of times."

"She wants you to be happy." Caitlyn's heart sped. Mitch was free.

He nestled her against his side again and her heart went into orbit.

If only she could count on him to keep himself safe.

Since neither Jared nor Caitlyn had ever visited the Alamo, Tara insisted they tour the ancient shrine to all that was the great state of Texas.

Mitch tagged along in the guise of making Caitlyn feel

safe. At least that gave him a reason to hover near. She'd left her crutches at the ranch but leaned heavily on the cane he'd gotten from Stan.

As they entered the hallowed ground where a small band of Texans had held out for thirteen days against Mexico's Santa Anna, Mitch removed his hat. Though he'd been there countless times, he saw the historical significance anew each time he visited.

A gray-haired lady led a group tour, giving a short history of the Texas revolution and how the Alamo had fallen, leading to the deaths of its famous defenders such as Davy Crockett, James Bowie, William Travis and Sam Houston.

"The shout, 'Remember the Alamo!' still resonates with Texans today." The guide's voice took on a passionate, reverent quality. "People worldwide continue to remember the Alamo as a heroic struggle against impossible odds—a place where men made the ultimate sacrifice for freedom. For this reason, the Alamo remains the Shrine of Texas Liberty."

The tour ended and the family broke away from the group. Quiet, each seemingly lost in their own thoughts of all they'd heard as they exited the stone structure.

"I'm glad you decided to stay for the wedding." He matched Caitlyn's stride. "I mean—it means a lot to Tara." *And me.*

She didn't say anything.

"You okay?"

"Fine. I just never realized the men's wives and children were also caught in the siege. They must have been so frightened."

"Yes, but they all got to return to their homes." He squeezed her shoulder. "Safe and sound."

"Next stop, the bridal shop for final fittings." Tara spun a circle on the sidewalk.

"A dress shop." Cody chuckled. "Think I'll pass and go on to the River Walk."

"Tara and Caitlyn are the only ones required for the fitting." Mom held Dad's hand as the walk symbol turned green and they crossed the street. "I already passed my test and Jared certainly doesn't need to see the dress. The rest of us could all head to the mall and meet up there."

"Think I'll escort the pretty ladies," Mitch offered.

He heard Caitlyn's breath catch, but she didn't protest.

The bell above the door dinged as they stepped inside the store. Rows of puffy dresses made of yards of cloud-like material and lace surrounded him.

"Ah, there's my bride." A trim lady in her sixties tucked Tara's hand in the crook of her elbow. "Is this the groom? No groom for the fitting. You mustn't see the dress."

"No." Tara laughed. "This is my brother. And this is my last-minute bridesmaid."

"In this day and age, do we really believe in bad luck?" Mitch quirked an eyebrow.

The bridal shop lady's mouth tightened in disapproval. "I take no chances when it comes to marriage. Come, ladies."

Tara shot him a behave-yourself glare and disappeared down a hall. Caitlyn followed without giving him so much as a glance.

He settled in one of several cushy white wing chairs facing a floor-to-ceiling mirror and raised platform. Nothing manly about this place. The end table beside the chair held several magazines. All bridal. He twiddled his thumbs.

The swish of fabric announced Tara's approach. He raised his head. White fluff everywhere. His little sister— a beautiful bride. "You look amazing."

"Really?" Her smile carried more wattage than all the

lighting in the store as she smoothed the dress and turned a circle in front of the mirrors.

"You'd better be glad I really like Jared."

"Isn't he the greatest?"

"Ahem." The bridal-shop lady clapped her hands. "Where is my bridesmaid?"

"The dress fits fine." Caitlyn's voice came from the back of the store.

"No, you must let me see. And you won't get the full effect without all the mirrors and lighting."

"Come on, Caitlyn. I want to see, too," Tara called.

A rustling sound and Caitlyn appeared in the hallway. His breath stalled. Her sleeveless lace dress in that purple-pink color his sister called fuchsia stopped just above shapely knees. The modest V neckline accented her collarbone.

"Turn," the bridal lady ordered.

As Caitlyn turned, he saw the V revealed a tantalizing expanse of her back.

"Oh, Caitlyn, I love it." Tara's excitement transferred to her tone.

"And a male perspective?" The bridal lady glanced in his direction.

"Borgeous." Mitch squeezed his eyes shut. "I mean—beautiful and gorgeous all wrapped up in one amazing wom—I mean, dress."

Caitlyn's face turned almost the shade of the dress.

"Is it me—" the bridal lady laughed "—or does the brother have a thing for the bridesmaid? Maybe another wedding in the works." She circled Caitlyn as Mitch's ears burned. "No alterations needed. Now let me concentrate on my bride."

Caitlyn hurried toward the back of the store.

Four more days to show her just how serious his thing for her was.

* * *

Sidewalks circled and twined around the mall. Caitlyn strolled along the River Walk with Tara, Jared and Cody. Mitch trailed behind with his mom, dad and grandfather.

If only the gentle lapping of the river alongside them would take her away. Let her forget Mitch's presence. Help her not need him.

She had to stop leaning on him. Her heart couldn't take his nearness. Especially since she now knew he wasn't seeing anyone else.

"I can't believe you've never been here." Tara paused as a boat packed with people passed. "We could ride a river taxi."

"That sounds fun." Caitlyn tried to take in all the sights, sounds and delicious smells emanating from restaurants.

"Maybe we can fit one in before lunch." Tara linked her arm through Caitlyn's.

"You sure? I don't want to cut into your shopping time."

"We'll have plenty of time." Tara waved a taxi over as it rounded a bend. "This is one of the stops."

The boat pulled alongside them and stopped.

"Let me help you." Mitch stepped into the boat and supported Caitlyn's weight as she boarded. His arms slipped naturally around her waist as he lifted her into the taxi. Her hands shook as they settled on his shoulders.

"I need to sit down." She had to get away from Mitch.

A young couple stood, creating a space wide enough for two at the front of the boat. "We'll move to the back so you won't have to."

"Thank you." Caitlyn claimed the seat and tried not to whack anyone with her cane. If only the woman had stayed, to keep Mitch from sitting beside her.

"How many tickets?" the driver inquired.

"Oh, you know, we'd better make it two." Tara smiled from the sidewalk.

"Two?" Caitlyn tried to hide the panic in her tone.

"Mom and I can shop. We'll need some male input, so the other men can go with us." Tara waved and the taxi pulled away.

Cody shrugged helplessly from the sidewalk.

"Well, that went according to her plan." Mitch grinned at his retreating family.

Warmth threaded through her at his smile. Too close. With a boatload of people, how could it feel as if they were alone?

"Were you in on this?" Caitlyn asked.

"Of course not." Mitch sighed and scanned the expanse of river in front of them. "But we've got a beautiful river. Let's enjoy it."

Caitlyn tried to relax, but his knee hovering inches from hers kept her heart stammering. They rounded a bend and her stomach didn't make the turn. "Oh, no."

"What?"

"Motion sickness." She closed her eyes, but her stomach spun more. "I need off."

"Driver!" Mitch cupped his hands around his mouth. "My friend is feeling sick. Could we stop?"

"Of course."

The boat neared the sidewalk, but it still seemed miles away. Bile rose in the back of her throat. Her flesh heated.

The boat stopped. Her stomach collided with the stillness and she stood. Her head swam. Mitch's arm came around her waist.

"I'm sorry for the extra stop," she apologized.

"Not a problem, ma'am." The driver tipped his straw hat. "Feel better."

Mitch picked her up. Someone handed him her cane and he stepped off the boat with his awkward bundle.

"Stop walking or I'm going to hurl all over you."

Mitch stopped.

"Set me down."

He did and she slid down to the sidewalk. Sitting in the middle of the cool concrete with people sidestepping her, she covered her face with both hands and sucked in deep, settling breaths while Mitch hovered at her side.

"You okay?"

"Just don't ever put me on a boat again." Finally, her stomach righted itself.

"Was that your first boat ride?"

"And last."

"I'm sorry, I should have known. You always got sick on the bus if you didn't sit up front."

"It seems to be worse the older I get. Tara will pay for this."

"What do you say we find a bench and while away the morning people watching?"

"That sounds nice." And still. Except for his company.

The rest of the week, wedding prep and two more shopping trips ate up Caitlyn's time, including several outings with Mitch hovering near. But with his entire family along each time, she'd managed to steer clear of any more alone time with him.

The day before the wedding, she stayed busy helping with decorations. Tulle, lace and flowers created a wedding wonderland in Grandpa's backyard, and the late-September forecast promised to be perfect. Just the rehearsal and wedding left to get through.

Family members and friends arrived steadily all day. As everyone pitched in with final details, Caitlyn got reacquainted with Mitch's cousin Clay and his wife, Rayna, the creative director for the Stockyards' publicity campaign.

No run-ins with Mitch all day. Not until they gathered in the backyard for rehearsal.

"Okay, how are the bridesmaids and groomsmen paired up?" the wedding planner asked.

Paired up? A tremor moved through Caitlyn. What happened to the old-fashioned way of having the groomsmen already at the front of the church as the bridal party walks down the aisle? Surely Mitch wasn't her escort. Tara wouldn't do that to her.

Tara's guilty gaze met Caitlyn's.

Yes. She would.

"You're with Mitch."

"What about the standby cousin?" Caitlyn heard the panic in her tone. "I assumed he'd be my escort."

"You're too tall for him, so we had to shift things around."

"Oh, sure you did."

"I love you." Tara hugged her.

"I can tell."

"If I didn't love you," Tara whispered, "I'd leave you alone and let you be miserable without my brother."

Mitch cleared his throat right behind her. "I'm told I'm your escort."

"Everything will work out perfect. You'll see." Tara let go of her and shoved her in Mitch's direction.

He offered his arm.

With no choice, Caitlyn rested her hand on his bicep. And shivered at his nearness.

Just get through this. Two more days and they'd go their separate ways.

Focus on his sister and her wedding day. But Mitch was hard-pressed to think about anything other than Caitlyn.

For the past several days, she'd pulled away from him. But last night, he'd walked down the aisle with her countless times and sat beside her at the rehearsal dinner. Today, he'd escort her along the white flowery runner he'd helped

Mom pin in place in the backyard. They'd flank the archway near the preacher.

But it wasn't their wedding. And at the rate he was going,
it never would be.

This was his last chance. After the wedding and reception, he'd see Tara and her new husband off and help with
the cleanup. Tomorrow morning, he'd drive Caitlyn home.
He had to do something. Today. To let her know how he
felt. If he didn't, she'd walk out of his life again.

"Wedding March" began, and the first two couples
walked the aisle. Their turn. Caitlyn's shaky hand rested
on his arm.

"You're safe," he whispered as they strode down the
aisle. Her pace was too fast, as if she wanted to get the
whole thing over with. "Slow down."

With a sigh, she slowed. Near the arch, where Jared
stood with the pastor, she started to pull her hand free, but
Mitch clamped his hand over hers.

As her startled gaze met his, he captured her chin with
his free hand and pressed a kiss on her silky cheek. He
heard her sharp intake of breath.

Her eyes got too shiny. Fast. She pulled away and fell in
line with the other bridesmaids.

If she didn't have any feelings for him anymore, why
would his kiss take her breath away? His heart almost burst
as he took his place with the other groomsmen. Why would
she be teary? His gaze stayed on her while she looked anywhere but at him. The "Wedding March" intensified with
the erratic beat of his heart.

Tara's cue to enter. Mitch forced his attention to his
sister—to share the happiest day of her life.

Tomorrow he'd concentrate on Caitlyn.

And who said he had to drive the speed limit? Driving
her home might be the slowest trip he'd ever made.

\* \* \*

Caitlyn helped Cody roll up the fabric aisle.

The newlyweds had left for the airport in San Antonio and were probably en route to their Florida honeymoon by now. All the guests had left and only the family remained in cleanup mode. Caitlyn pitched in while trying to keep her distance from Mitch.

Under the archway that still mocked her, he'd kissed her goodbye. He knew as well as she did that they had no future. She could still feel the warmth of his lips on her cheek. Tears singed her eyes. If she kept thinking about it, she'd turn into a blubbering idiot.

"Hello?" Cody's voice caught her attention.

"Huh?"

"I'm no expert at such things, but don't you think we should do better than this?"

The runner was wadded and diagonal. She backed away from Cody, unrolling to start the process over. "Sorry."

"That kiss got you flustered?"

"I can't talk about it. Or him."

He held up one hand. "Sorry."

Paying attention this time, she rolled the runner, keeping the edges straight.

With the roll finished and much neater, Cody took it from her. "Take a coffee break. I put a fresh pot on."

"That sounds awesome." She headed for the house. "I'll bring you a cup."

Just inside the kitchen door, she saw him. Mitch was staring at the small TV by the breakfast bar.

"As soon as we have more information, we'll report it," the reporter droned. "Again, Flight 217 has disappeared from radar. Apparently, the pilot radioed the control tower due to engine problems and attempted an emergency landing." The newscaster's solemn tone turned her insides.

"However, since the flight was bound for Florida, most of the flight plan was over the gulf."

Bound for Florida? Surely not Tara's flight. *Lord, please no.* Caitlyn gasped.

Mitch turned to face her. Alarm filled his gaze.

The moonlight cast an eerie glow through Caitlyn's curtains. Wide-awake, she checked the digital clock on her nightstand—3:27 a.m.

Not wanting to impose, her insides quivered. But she was dying to go downstairs.

She threw back the covers, flipped the light on and dressed. Imposition or not, she couldn't stay here, not knowing a minute longer.

All evening, tension had increased as phone calls to Tara and Jared's cells went unanswered. A call to the hotel in Florida revealed the couple hadn't arrived at their destination.

Mitch tried calling the airport and had gotten the all-lines-are-busy message. Finally, Mitch, Cody and Grandpa had gone to the airport.

A vehicle had returned a few minutes ago.

Soundlessly, she crept down the stairs. Was that the sound of crying? Audra and Wayne in the living room. Her eyes stung and she cut to the right, escaping into the darkened kitchen.

A large shape sat hunched on the island countertop. Caitlyn quenched a gasp and started to back out of the room. But her eyes adjusted to the moonlight. Mitch, his face in his hands, his shoulders shaking.

Her heart turned over as she hurried to him and slipped her arms around his shoulders. He stilled for a moment.

"It's okay. Let it out."

He slid off the counter to his feet, pulling her tight, his sobs rocking them both.

Minutes passed. He quieted. The shaking stopped.

"With all the wedding fuss, they didn't give us their flight number. But we're pretty sure it was their plane." Anguish echoed in his tone. "It was the only flight to Florida tonight."

"Maybe they decided to go somewhere else."

"It's our only hope. The airport will have the passenger list in the morning."

"What about Jared's family?"

"They haven't heard from them, either."

"Have they found the plane?" Her voice trembled.

"In the gulf. No survivors so far." He cleared his throat. "I need to get back in there with my family. I just needed a minute."

"You don't have to be strong for them."

"Thanks for being my shoulder." His hand cupped her cheek.

"I love Tara, too." Her vision blurred and she blinked.

"I know." He kissed her temple, then pulled away to look at her. His gaze caught on her lips.

As if drawn by a magnet, Caitlyn stretched up on tiptoe to oblige him. Their lips met and her arms twined around his neck. Ten years of missing, longing and regretting exploded between them.

## Chapter 9

"Whoa!" Cody's surprise sounded in his tone.

She and Mitch sprang apart.

"Uh, sorry. Didn't mean to interrupt." Cody backed out of the room.

Turning her back on him, Caitlyn pressed her hand to her quivering lips.

"I—"

"We're both upset." Her voice quivered, too. "We're not thinking rationally. Go on. Your family needs you."

He took a few steps, then stopped. "I may not be able to take you home tomorrow. You might need to call Natalie or your dad."

"Don't worry about me."

He left her alone and Caitlyn gripped the countertop so hard her fingers went numb.

Ten years of trying to get over Mitch, and one kiss froze her brain. She couldn't do this again. He still had a dangerous job.

And Caitlyn had to let him go.

What kind of person was she? Thinking about Mitch and their future when Tara's life hung in the balance.

Mitch drummed his fingers on the kitchen counter. It was still early, but he wanted to get to the airport.

Doubtful anyone in the house had slept, he tried to remain quiet. He certainly hadn't slept a wink, but he welcomed the distraction of the kiss. Anything to stop worrying about his sister. The kiss would make Tara happy. She'd wanted him to get back with Caitlyn for ten years.

Maybe at the airport they'd learn Tara and Jared weren't on that plane. And maybe that kiss could help him win Caitlyn back. And give his sister a happy ending when she came home. If she came home.

No, he couldn't think that way.

The shrill ring of the phone cut through the silence.

The airport? This early? Was it good news? *Please, Lord, let it be.*

He grabbed the handset. "Hello?"

"Mitch, it's Tara."

Spasms exploded through his chest. "Where are you?"

"We're at the Hilton in San Antonio. We were tired last night and changed our flight. We weren't on that plane."

Tears rained down his cheeks, and his throat clogged. "We tried to call you."

"I know. I'm sorry. It was our wedding night, so we turned our phones off. We didn't know about the crash until this morning."

"You're okay? Both of you?"

"We're fine. And I think we're questioning getting on a plane. We may drive to Florida. Take our time, stop when we want and sightsee."

"That sounds like an awesome plan."

Mom and Dad careened into the kitchen, followed by

Cody and Grandpa. Mitch gave them a thumbs-up. "It's Tara. They're fine. They weren't on the flight."

Tears of relief swept over the family. Caitlyn stopped in the doorway, looking as if she felt out of place.

"They're okay." Cody wrapped her up in a bear hug.

"Let me talk to her." Dad reached for the phone.

"Put her on speakerphone." Mom's voice quivered.

Mitch gave the handset to his father, walked over to Caitlyn and stole her from his brother's arms. A whirlpool of emotions swept through him and the only person he wanted to share it with was Caitlyn. She clung to him.

"We should pray for the families who did have loved ones on that plane." Cody massaged Mom's shoulders. "We know exactly what they're going through."

"Good idea, son."

"Hey, Daddy. We're fine." Tara's reassuring voice boomed over the speaker.

A collective sigh of relief swept through the kitchen.


"We're here." Mitch's voice came from far away. "Caitlyn, you're home."

She opened her eyes, squinting in the late-afternoon sun. Her dollhouse. Home.

"Sorry, I guess I slept the whole trip."

"I imagine you're exhausted."

"You, too."

"I'll be all right. It's only an hour to Garland."

"I don't know what to say. Thanks doesn't seem to cover it."

"I'm just glad you're okay."

"I'm glad Tara's okay."

"Me, too." He opened his door. "Looks like your family has spotted us."

Mama, Daddy and Natalie scurried toward her side of the truck. Before she could say another word, her door was open and Daddy was scooping her out. Her family huddled around her in a group hug.

"So happy you're home safe." Mama's words came through tears.

"Ditto." Natalie hugged her again.

They drew her toward the house and Daddy turned toward Mitch. "Thank you."

"Just doing my job."

It had only been his job. Caitlyn's heart took a dive. His very dangerous job. He dealt with stalkers, and worse, daily. The past two weeks had been an emotional roller coaster and had reawakened old feelings for both of them.

But they were still at an impasse. Mitch loved his job. And even though he wasn't seeing someone new, his job left no room for Caitlyn in his life.

Just one final glimpse of him. She turned, but he was already in his truck. The engine started and he drove away without so much as a wave.

Surreal. Home—her dollhouse. It was her graduation gift—a smaller version of Mama and Daddy's home and a twin to Natalie's. As she climbed the steps up the porch, it seemed like months had passed since she'd been here instead of only two weeks.

She hugged herself.

"Relax, pumpkin, it's over. You're home." Daddy shot her a wink.

The white-columned porch felt almost alien. Inside, the pale terra-cotta tile and walls, creamy leather sofa and bronze horse sculptures seemed almost unfamiliar. She held her breath, scanning the room as if some stalker hid behind the curtains.

"Are you sure you don't want to stay with us tonight?" Mama squeezed her elbow.

"No, I'm fine."

"Lane and I could spend the night with you." Natalie plopped on the couch.

"Really, I'm fine. Just tired." Even though she'd slept the entire five hours home. Exhausted—from dealing with a stalker. But mostly from dealing with Mitch.

"We'll let you get some rest, then." Daddy patted her arm.

One more group hug and her family filed out.

Caitlyn sank into the sofa, pressed a pillow to her stomach and curled her knees up under her chin. The throw on the back of the couch cushioned her cheek in an intricate southwest pattern woven together in shades of terra-cotta, jade and sea foam that reminded her of Mitch's eyes. She pulled the throw around her.

Cold. Scared. And lonely for Mitch.

A stalker, Mitch back in her life, an attack, a five-hour drive with Mitch, a wound, an infection, Mitch constantly hovering, falling in love with his family again, a suicide, a wedding, Tara in potential danger, a kiss and a second five-hour drive with Mitch. All within sixteen days.

And now she was supposed to get back to normal.

Without him.


Aubrey's Main Street teemed with people. Many Caitlyn knew, many she didn't. Vendor booths lined the streets and the field in front of the old peanut dryer selling crafts, quilts, peanut-themed food and hand-carved items. She'd always loved the Peanut Festival in October. Until today.

This week had definitely been calmer than the previous one. She'd run her store on autopilot.

But her fears had closed in on her back at the scene of the crime. At least there weren't any gunfight reenactments at the Stockyards this time of year. It would be embarrassing to hit the dirt at the sound of a fake gunshot.

Thank goodness her doctor insisted she rest her leg for

another week before resuming her rodeo-queen duties. She'd let her boss down, but thoughts of the rodeo almost gave her a panic attack.

But the doctor had said she could ride in the parade. And riding her horse in the Peanut Festival Parade might be her undoing.

Her hands shook as she stood beside Lightning, gripping the reins. She scanned the face of each man in the crowd.

"Caitlyn." Mitch's voice came from directly behind her. She jumped and spun around to face him.

"Sorry. Didn't mean to sneak up on you."

He looked way too handsome in his cream-colored ranger hat, white shirt with lone-star appliqués and dark jeans. Caitlyn's insides melted. "I have to get Lightning lined up for the parade."

"I'm riding with you."

"What?"

"I called Natalie to check on you. She said you're having a rough time and seemed jumpy about the parade. So I arranged to ride with you. Thought I might make you feel safe."

Her nerves settled. How could he make her feel physically safe and emotionally terrified at the same time?

"Is that okay with you?"

"Thank you." She closed her eyes.

"Want me to be at the rodeo tonight, too?"

"I'm not supposed to go back until next week, but don't you have to work?"

"I'm off duty on weekends for two months. I can be at every rodeo if you want."

"I want." Her chin wobbled and she hugged him.

His arms came around her. Felt so good. So strong. So safe.

So threatening.

\* \* \*

Peanuts littered Main Street as Mitch walked Caitlyn to her car.

Her red-white-and-blue-spangled jacket was blinding in the sun, and her eyes were bright.

"I haven't been to the Peanut Festival in years." Good memories. Of home. Of Caitlyn.

"I'm glad you came." Her hand brushed his and she jerked away.

"Me, too." If only they could walk hand in hand through the rest of their lives. He cleared his throat. "So how are you? Really."

"I jump at my own shadow." Her sigh sounded heavy. "My parents hover. Natalie's scheduled me for tons of speaking engagements and public appearances, but just going to my store scares me to death."

"The danger's over, Cait. One step at a time. You're safe."

"I don't feel safe." She closed her eyes.

"Stuart is dead. He can't hurt you."

"No, but what if there's another Stuart? I have to face Cowtown next week."

"You'll have to face the darkened seats of the arena. Among strangers and crowds."

"And crowds of strangers." She shivered.

"You've been through a traumatic experience. I understand, but I won't let you crawl inside yourself."

"I feel like there's someone waiting for me behind every shadow. You can't understand."

"Oh, but I do. I've seen it. I've lived it. The first time I faced a real assailant with a real gun instead of a cardboard cutout in training, I jumped at my own shadow for weeks."

"Really?"

"Even Texas Rangers in the making get scared. Still do."

"I know it's not logical." She huffed out a sigh. "I mean,

in all my twenty-eight years this was the first time anyone ever stalked me. This man homed in on me because I
look like his wife. Odds are, this will never happen again."

"But logic has nothing to do with how you feel."

"I'm not sure I'll ever feel really safe again." She hugged
herself. "How do I get past it?"

He'd give anything to hug her. Instead, he captured her
hand.

"One step at a time. And I might be able to help with
step one." He squeezed her hand. "I visited Stevens's son
this week. To thank him for working with us. He feels terrible for what his dad did to you and he'd like to meet you
and apologize."

"None of it was his fault."

"I know that and you know that, but he still feels responsible."

"And you think my meeting him would help him."

"And you. This may sound crazy, but maybe talking
things through could get you both past everything that happened."

"I'll think about it." She pressed her clicker and her lights
flashed. "Here's my car."

"I'll see you at the rodeo next week. What about your
horse? How do you get her to the rodeo?"

"Lane brings her in his trailer with his horse. I really
appreciate everything you've done."

"No problem." He tipped his hat as she got in her car
and started the engine.

She'd softened over the past three weeks. When he'd
initially seen her at Cowtown, she'd been so anxious to
be rid of him she'd ditched him and put herself in danger.
Even when he'd first taken her to Medina, she'd wanted
to avoid him.

But now she welcomed his company. As long as he didn't

get too close. Out of fear, but he'd take it. Could there still be a chance for them?

There had to be. The past week without seeing her had been torture, and he couldn't face an entire lifetime without her. Why had he ever thought he could?

For the first time since the attack, Caitlyn sat astride Lightning at Cowtown Coliseum. Her nerve endings danced, even though Mitch stood beside her. Come to think of it, he was probably part of the reason for her nervousness. She gripped the reins tighter.

"You're fine." He patted her booted foot. "I'm right here and I've got a loaded gun."

She laughed. "And that's supposed to make me feel safe. I'm terrified of guns."

"So are the bad guys." He shot her a wink.

And her heart went into orbit.

The music began—"God Bless the U.S.A." Another deep breath and she relaxed a bit. She gently dug her heels in Lightning's sides and the horse shot into the arena.

Stuart Stevens was not out there watching her. But was someone else? She shook her head. Even if someone else was out there, Mitch was here. He'd keep her safe.

"I'm safe. I'm safe. I'm safe." The ridiculous mantra calmed her as the song came to a climax and she urged Lightning to charge around the arena as they'd done countless times before.

And before she knew it, she'd carried her final flag of the evening, her duties done as the rodeo wound down.

Mitch waited for her at the gate and it took everything she had to keep from diving into his arms as he helped her dismount. He gripped her gently by both shoulders and turned her to face him.

"You're okay."

"Thanks." She nodded. "I'm really not sure I could have worked tonight if you weren't here."

"Glad to be of service, ma'am."

His cowboy charm almost did her in. As her heart raced, she tried to think of something other than him. "I've been thinking."

"Yes."

"I think I'd like to meet with Stevens's son."

"I'll contact him about setting up a meeting and call you. With his class schedule, it will probably have to be on a weekend."

If she didn't know better, she'd say disappointment dwelled in his eyes.

Had he thought she'd been thinking about their future? Truth be told, she had. But no matter how many times her heart and brain spun with possibilities, they had no future.

"Four rodeos down. You did great the past two weekends." Mitch opened the door to Caitlyn's store and held it for her. The bell dinged as they stepped outside to the crowded brick streets of the Stockyards.

"I still don't think I could have done it without your gun there." Caitlyn sighed. "I don't know what I'll do when you start having to work weekends again."

"By then you'll be back to normal, not a care in the world." He hoped. It tore at his soul to see fear in her eyes. Even though her fear kept him around.

"I don't even remember not having a care in the world."

He touched her hand, expecting her to jerk away.

But she didn't.

Encouraged, he threaded his fingers through hers.

She let him.

Progress. He smiled.

"So are you sure this kid isn't anything like his dad?" Her hand trembled beneath his.

"Nothing whatsoever." He gave her fingers a reassuring squeeze. "The man who bought my folks' ranch got guardianship of him until he started college. He's a Christian and he's studying to be a vet."

"Quinn Remington. A good man. Sounds like Stevens's son broke away from his father's shadow." Her hand trembled again. "How did they catch Stevens? You never told me."

"I set up his son as a lure at Quinn's place. After Stevens left his brother's house, he went there."

"You put his son in danger?" Her hand stiffened in his. "Not to mention his guardian."

"Relax. The place was crawling with rangers. When Stevens showed up, they were waiting for him. He caught on and ran to the next ranch, but there were too many civilians in the area to make a safe arrest."

"And folks think nothing ever happens in Aubrey."

"Most folks never knew anything was going on." He squeezed her hand again. "Stevens stole a truck and rangers followed at a distance until he stopped at an abandoned rental house in Fort Worth, where he'd apparently been living. You know the rest."

"It must have been very hard on his son to set him up like that."

"He didn't want his father to hurt anyone else." He led her across the street toward Cowtown Coliseum.

"We're meeting with him here?"

"I thought, since this is where the whole thing started, meeting with Trent here might ease some fears. I'll be close the whole time." He squeezed her hand again.

"Don't you have anything else to do when you're not working other than babysit me?"

"Nope. And it's my pleasure." He stopped at the steps. "Ready?"

She nodded and her grip tightened.

He could get used to this. If only it didn't take fear to convince her to put up with him.

A whole swarm of butterflies did somersaults in Caitlyn's stomach. What if Stevens's death had triggered some kind of rage in his son? What if he blamed her for his dad's death? What if he looked like his dad—the face that haunted her dreams?

But Mitch was with her. He'd keep her safe. And her safety might endanger him.

The greeter, Lonnie, dressed in cowboy gear provided by her store, stood at his post by the door of Cowtown. "Afternoon, Caitlyn. You're in early."

"I'm meeting with someone."

"I believe he's here. Young fella was asking about you."

"Asking about me?" Her stomach took a dive.

"Just if you were here yet."

Mitch squeezed her hand.

"Oh. Okay, thanks. We'll find him."

As they stepped inside the lobby out of the bright sunlight, she couldn't see a thing other than spots for a minute or two. Her eyes adjusted slowly. A dark shape took form and walked toward her. She gasped.

The boy gasped, too. "I didn't realize how much you look like my mother. I mean—the last time I saw her, anyway."

At least the boy seemed harmless—apprehensive, but not threatening in the least. And, thank goodness, he didn't look like his father. Same height, but his face and body were fuller. His hair was much darker, his eyes were a vivid pool-blue and, most important, his eyes were kind.

"This is Caitlyn Wentworth. Caitlyn, meet Trent Stevens."

A group of tourists entered.

"Let's go to the dressing room." Caitlyn dug the key out of her purse.

The hair along the back of her neck stood on end. Since that last letter, she'd been unable to walk through Cowtown without feeling that someone was watching her. Even with Mitch trailing her.

She unlocked the dressing room and ushered both men inside.

"I'm sorry—for my dad. Sorry is nothing after what he did to you. But—"

"It's not your fault." Her voice trembled, but at least she'd managed to speak.

"Somehow, I thought meeting you—telling you how sorry I am—I thought it might make me feel better." His shoulders slumped and his gaze dropped to the floor. "But, I don't know what to say to you. Sorry doesn't seem like enough."

"You have nothing to be sorry about. Why don't you tell me about you? Your life? Your mom? If you want to, that is. Here, I'll start."

She gave him a short summation of her life, leaving out any mention of scary letters or his father.

"You might know Quinn—the man who saved my life." Trent settled in a folding chair, his eyes on the floor.

"I know Quinn through the rodeo. And his wife. Lacie has shopped in my store for years." The world seemed to keep getting smaller. "They're good people. I'm glad they were able to help you."

"My life with them is like light compared to dark." He picked at a hole in the knee of his jeans. "For as long as I can remember, my dad hit my mom. He always threatened to kill her if she left. And especially if she tried to take me with her."

Caitlyn touched his hand.

"I kind of thought it was normal, I guess." He hiked up

one shoulder. "Until I got in church and saw how men treat women. I didn't become a Christian until I was seventeen, and by then I'd made a lot of mistakes."

"It doesn't sound like you had an example to go by."

"I didn't. But that's no excuse. I took advantage of girls and got one pregnant."

"You have a child?" She tried to keep the shock out of her voice. He was so young.

"By the time the girl learned she was pregnant, I had a new girlfriend, so she gave our baby girl up for adoption. I know the adoptive parents." His voice caught. "I've watched her grow up—from a distance. It's hard to stay out of her life sometimes, but she's happy."

"You're very wise for your age."

"Her parents promised to tell her who I am when she gets a little older."

"They sound very wise, too."

"They are." A thread gave way and the hole in his jeans got bigger. "I have a girlfriend at school. She's a Christian and we're honoring God in our relationship, but her dad hates me."

"Why? I just met you, but you seem like a great guy."

"He knows about my past, so he thinks I'm bad news."

"Just give it time." She patted his shoulder. "Time will prove you're worthy of his daughter."

"That's what I've been doing, but so far I'm not getting anywhere with him."

"You're right to honor her father. But don't ever give up on love."

Caitlyn glanced at Mitch. Exactly what she'd done—given up on love.

"Did I honor my father? I mean, I testified against him and put him in jail."

"You kept him from hurting you or anyone else." For a while, anyway.

"It didn't help you."

"It's over now." She said it with more conviction than she felt.

"I'm glad. I was going to testify against him again in your case. But now that will never happen."

"I'm sorry." Her gaze dropped to the floor.

"I'm not. I was dreading facing him again. Part of me is glad I won't ever have to."

"I've felt the same way." Caitlyn's voice quivered. "And then I feel guilty. I'm a Christian. I shouldn't be glad someone's dead."

She looked up. Trent stared at her. Her stomach twisted. Had her honesty made him angry?

"I'm sorry. You can't imagine how much you look like my mom."

"Do you have a picture of her?"

"I do." Trent fished his wallet out and handed her a worn photo.

Same facial shape, coloring and long dark hair.

Caitlyn gasped. "How long ago was this taken?"

"I was seven."

And now he was eighteen—making his mom the right age. Could it be? "I think your mom might be my missing aunt."

# Chapter 10

Why hadn't Mitch ever thought to mention the possible family connection to Caitlyn? Such a strong resemblance must mean a blood tie, but he'd gotten so caught up in Caitlyn he'd forgotten all about Camille.

Had the meeting been a good idea? Caitlyn clung to Mitch's hand during the walk back to her store. Quiet. Too quiet. Her heels clicking against the brick streets was the only sound she made.

He cleared his throat. "You okay?"

"Just shaken."

"Why did you never mention your missing aunt to me? Even back when we were…"

"I knew the mystery would intrigue you, and it upsets Mama to talk about it." She shrugged. "Should I tell her Trent's mother is probably her missing sister? I don't want to get her hopes up."

"Let's do some research first. I can check our cold-case database. What was her maiden name?"

"Prentiss. Millie Prentiss."

"You got a minute? My laptop's in the truck right over there."

"The store's in good hands. Let's go."

For the first time since her attack, fire returned to her eyes, blotting out the fear. Maybe her aunt's disappearance could redirect her focus.

Caitlyn walked beside him with her old independent, confident poise. No looking over her shoulder.

*Lord, please help her recover.*

He never thought he'd miss her stubborn determination, but he did. He unlocked his truck. "The database is top secret."

"No problem." She crossed her arms over her chest and leaned back against his truck bed. "Just tell me if Trent's mom is my aunt."

Mitch pulled up the missing persons cold cases and typed in Millie Prentiss. A file popped up. Camille Prentiss. He opened it. A picture of Trent's mom stared at him. Disappeared at sixteen without a trace on March 17, thirty years ago. Rumors of a possessive, older boyfriend at Cowtown Coliseum, where she was last seen. Her family reported Millie had never come home from the rodeo where she'd competed as a barrel racer.

"Anything?" Anxiety rang in Caitlyn's tone.

A tap of the mouse enlarged the picture to fill the screen. He stepped out of his truck. "This is Camille Prentiss, also known as Millie."

Caitlyn's hand flew to her mouth. "Of course. Why didn't I realize before? Mama always shortens people's names. She calls me Caitie. Natalie is Nattie."

"Camille. Millie. And Stevens shortened it to Cammie."

"Stevens was the possessive boyfriend."

"Probably." He flipped the laptop shut. "My guess is he

forced her to leave with him. I'm going to headquarters to officially open her cold case."

"Thank you." She closed her eyes.

"We'll do our best to find her."

"What if he killed her?"

"Don't think that way." He cupped her cheek in his hand.

"I don't want to, but she's been gone for thirty years. If she left him, why didn't she come home?"

"Because he threatened to find her and kill her. She wouldn't have gone anywhere obvious. And she wouldn't have done anything to endanger her family."

"You really think she's alive?"

"Stevens has several crimes on his record—mostly assault and battery. But he never killed anyone—that we know of."

"He certainly tried to do me in." She shivered.

"It could be argued that your wounds were self-defense." Mitch pulled her into his arms. "He probably wished he'd never tangled with this wildcat. Try to think positive."

"But I don't want to get my hopes up, just in case." She pulled away from him. "What about my mother—do I tell her?"

"Opening up a thirty-year-old missing-persons cold case in the wake of the death of the victim's husband will probably hit the papers. You might want to prepare her. Want me to go with you?"

"Could you?"

He grinned. "Just tell me when."

"I work right up until rodeo time tonight. How about tomorrow morning?"

"Done. In the meantime, I'll be back later to head to the rodeo with you."

"I really appreciate you." She checked her watch. "Better get back to the store. I've been so distracted—I have to focus."

"One step at a time." He tucked her hand in the crook of his elbow.

And he'd be there for each step.

Columns lined the porch on a bigger version of her own dollhouse next door. Caitlyn hurried toward her parents' house, trying to keep some space between her and Mitch for a change. She had to pull herself together. Stop leaning on him. Stop holding his hand. Stop loving him.

His hand grazed hers.

"Any updates on Millie?" She crossed her arms over her chest.

"We just opened the investigation. Give it some time."

"So what's being done? An all-points bulletin? What?"

"Impressive with the lingo."

"I watch cop shows." She shrugged. "I never dreamed my life would mirror one."

"But that's over now. And we're focusing on your aunt and moving forward."

"Right. One step at a time."

He followed her up the porch steps. "We put out an APB, but with a case this old, I doubt we'll get leads. So we flooded newspapers with Stevens's obituary. All over Texas and surrounding states. If your aunt learns he's not a threat anymore, maybe she'll come home."

"That's brilliant."

"Thanks." He tipped his hat.

"I can't stop thinking about Trent's daughter."

"So not only do you have a cousin you just met, but a second cousin somewhere near."

"It's a lot to take in." She turned from the house and scanned the Texas sky as if the answers were there. "I don't think I'll tell my family about his daughter yet. They'd want to know where she is, want to see her, and it would only complicate things for Trent. I think he's got enough complications as it is."

"Your call. Not a word from me."

She opened her parents' ornate door and called, "Mama? Daddy?"

"Come in, Caitie. It's open," her mom called.

Deep breath. Try to calm the nerves dancing due to her aunt's possible return and dealing with Mitch. She stepped inside.

"Hey, sis." Natalie met her in the foyer with a hug and let out a squeal when she noticed Mitch. "I knew it."

"What?"

"Y'all are back together. That's what the big family meeting is about. Oh, I'm so happy for you both." Natalie turned her loose and hugged Mitch.

"No, Natalie." Caitlyn gave an emphatic shake of her head. "We're not."

"You're not?" Natalie let go of Mitch.

He shot Caitlyn a mischievous grin.

"We're not back together." She focused on her sister.

"Oh. Well, this is awkward." Natalie sucked in her cheeks. "But it's only a matter of time. Y'all might as well stop fighting it. True love always wins."

Caitlyn's face heated.

"Same old Natalie." Mitch shoved his hands in his pockets.

"I hope not." Natalie shivered.

"I just meant—you say whatever you think."

"Oh, that." Natalie waved a dismissive hand.

"Part of her charm." Lane joined them and pulled his wife against his side. "You always know where you stand with this one."

"Lane, you remember Mitch Warren, the love of Caitlyn's life."

Steam would surely blow out of Caitlyn's ears any minute. She glared at her sister.

Natalie shot her a smile, linked arms with Caitlyn and headed toward the great room. "Mama and Daddy are waiting."

"Will you please let up?" Caitlyn whispered. "Before I die of embarrassment."

"I remember a time when I tried to avoid Lane. We were at Moms on Main and he came in. Guess who invited him to eat with us, then suddenly had to leave? Aren't paybacks fun?" Natalie squeezed her arm. "Besides, look at Lane and me now. Maybe Mitch came back into your life for a reason."

"I love you, in spite of your jackhammer subtlety."

"Right back at you—except you're about as subtle as they come. That's why you need me around to jump-start things."

"What are y'all up to?" Lane caught up with them. "That's an awful lot of whispering."

"Nothing." The sisters' voices blended.

Despite Mitch's presence, Caitlyn needed to focus. Maybe it hadn't been a good idea to invite him for moral support, after all. But she hoped Mama would handle the news better coming from him with his stoic ranger calm. And maybe even find hope.

Mitch cleared his throat. Relax. But he couldn't. Not in this showplace filled with antiques and expensive furniture. It was beautiful, but he was afraid to touch anything, much less sit on the fancy Queen Anne furnishings. Her parents' stuffy home didn't fit their down-to-earth personalities.

How to give Caitlyn's mom hope without getting her hopes up? "Maybe y'all should sit down."

The family lined up on the fancy white sofa, Caitlyn in

the middle, with Lane and Natalie and her parents flanking each side of her.

"Have a seat, Mitch." Daniel gestured to a matching chair across from them.

"I don't want to muss it."

"Claire loves collecting antiques." Daniel laughed. "But she firmly believes they should be enjoyed by using them."

Mitch sat.

"Just spill, Mitch." Claire clasped her trembling hands together. "You're making me a nervous wreck. Is this about Caitie's case? The man shot himself. It's over, isn't it?"

"Yes. It's over." His gaze met Caitlyn's and she shuddered. He hated bringing up Stevens again when she needed to forget he ever existed. "But there's a new development. In the course of the investigation, some facts came to light."

"Facts about what?" Daniel frowned.

"As you know, Caitlyn's attacker was a man named Stuart Stevens. Have any of y'all ever heard that name before Caitlyn's attack?" Mitch scanned each family member for any signs of recognition, especially Claire. Nothing.

"No." Their voices blended in unison.

"Stevens was married and had a son." Mitch leaned forward. "He physically abused his wife until she left him. Then he turned on his son."

"That's terrible. But what does this have to do with Caitlyn?" Natalie shrugged.

"This may come as a shock." Mitch took a deep breath and locked eyes with Claire. "But Stevens's missing wife is your missing sister."

Several gasps echoed through the room.

"Are you sure?" Claire's question came out in a tremulous whisper.

"Show her the picture, Mitch." Caitlyn clutched her mom's hand.

"Brace yourselves." He opened his briefcase and set his

laptop on the coffee table, then pulled up the file on Stevens and filled the screen with the picture Trent had given them. Slowly, he turned the computer to let Claire see.

Claire's hand flew to her mouth. "That's Millie."

"Stevens's son, Trent, gave us the picture. Your sister never mentioned Stevens?"

"No." Claire shook her head. "I never knew she was seeing anyone. It was just a rumor around the arena after she disappeared."

"So you think this man became obsessed with Caitlyn because he thought she was Millie?" Daniel rubbed his chin.

"Yes."

"He called me Camille, the night of my attack." Caitlyn's tone sent chills through him. "But I didn't know Aunt Millie's name was Camille. And I asked Nat not to tell y'all the details of the letters. I didn't want to upset y'all any further."

"Do you think Millie's alive?" Claire's eyes filled with hope.

"All we know is that she left Stevens twelve years ago." The light in Claire's eyes dimmed.

"But we're reopening her missing person's case."

"Please find her." Claire perked up again.

"We'll do the best we can. But I'll be honest. It's been thirty years. That makes it tough."

"So this man kidnapped Millie, forced her to marry him and have his child—" Daniel shook his head "—then beat her?"

"We're not sure if he took her by force or if she left willingly. She may have been young and in love. If there was a marriage before she turned eighteen, it wasn't legal, especially if she used a fake name."

"No." Claire stood and paced the room. "Millie would have never left her family by choice. Her disappearance killed our parents. Daddy grieved himself to death and

Mama's heart gave out. Millie would have never put us through this. And to leave her son behind? It doesn't sound like Millie."

Daniel met his wife midpace. "Violence and fear can make people do things they normally wouldn't."

"He may have threatened to hurt her family." If only Mitch could have kept all of this quiet until Camille was found. What if she was dead and he'd opened all these emotions up for nothing? "And we know he threatened to kill her if she took his son away."

"Mitch will find her, Mama." Caitlyn stood and hugged her mom. "One way or another."

Her gaze locked with his. Her family probably thought she meant whether Camille had left by force or willingly. But Mitch knew she meant alive or dead.

*Please let Camille be alive, Lord.* Stuart Stevens had put Caitlyn and her family through enough torment.

"Wait a minute—Millie has a son." Claire's eyes lit up again. "My nephew… He gave you the picture, so you know where he is. I want to see him."

"He's shaken by everything, but I'll talk to him about it."

"You'll keep us posted on the investigation?" Daniel asked.

"Of course." Mitch tipped his hat, feeling dismissed.

"I'll walk you out." Caitlyn hurried past him to the front of the house and opened the door for him.

"You think she's okay?" His fingers settled on her elbow.

"I hope so. You were very reassuring."

"I tried, but I know it was a shock. I only hope I can reunite your family."

"If Millie's alive, you'll find her. Thank you. I mean, you've gone above and beyond your call—keeping me safe and now reopening Millie's case."

"Aw, shucks, just doing my ranger duty, ma'am." He winked to make light of the subject.

But she didn't lighten up. The intensity in her eyes deepened. "Do you ever wish...?"

*We were together?* "Yes."

She blinked. "Then why don't you quit?"

Obviously, she hadn't been asking what he'd thought. "What was the question?"

"Do you ever wish you weren't a ranger? You know, let someone else get the bad guys while you live a normal life."

A knot hardened in his chest. "No. I've never wished I wasn't a ranger. Can't you see what Texas would be like without rangers?"

"Well, yes, but I mean let other people be rangers. Instead of you."

He frowned and shook his head. "I can't imagine doing anything else."

"Oh." Her gaze dropped to the floor. "Um, I guess you'd better go."

"I'll be at your store at six-thirty."

"Sure. Thanks. And thanks for breaking the news to Mama for me."

"No problem." He stepped outside and hurried down the steps toward his truck.

Frustration balled up in his chest. The problem was, he loved Caitlyn Wentworth. He'd never stopped. But he still couldn't have her because of the job he loved.

And oaf that he was, he kept wrangling ways to stay in her life and torture himself.

As he climbed in his truck, his phone rang. Timmons.

"Warren here."

"Mitch, I just got news your transfer went through. Come January when Barker retires, you'll be our new forensic artist."

*Thank You, Lord.* Something in his chest blossomed. Relief. "That's awesome!"

"We'll miss you on the beat, but I know you'll do great work."

"Thanks for letting me know." He hung up and turned back toward her parents' house. His job wouldn't keep them apart now. Surely, with his transfer, she'd let him close to her.

But, what if he didn't like the job or wasn't good at it? What then? Would she bolt?

His steps faltered.

No. He needed her to love him and accept him no matter what job he had. Now and in the future.

Rodeos, the store and the investigation took every bit of Caitlyn's energy—plus speaking engagements and photo shoots for Natalie's Cowtown ad campaign. But despite all the distractions, fear still reigned in the recesses of her brain.

Except when Mitch was around.

And he'd be here any minute to escort her across two hundred yards of brick-lined streets to Cowtown. Ridiculous. The fear keeping him in her life had become a delicious form of torture.

She turned off the lights and stared out the glass storefront. The usual crowd milled about. No one noticed her.

Not in the safety of her store. But the first week of November was already gone. Mitch would start working weekends in a matter of weeks. What would she do then?

Why couldn't she get past this? She wasn't some whimpering ninny. She'd taken self-defense classes. When Stuart Stevens had attacked her, she'd gotten away. And she'd hurt him badly enough that he'd sought medical attention. Which had led him to his end. Stuart Stevens was dead. He couldn't hurt her anymore.

Besides, he hadn't randomly chosen her to obsess over.

He'd mistaken her for his wife, who happened to be her aunt. What were the odds of that ever happening again?

*I'm safe. I'm safe. I'm safe.*

Caitlyn took a deep breath and opened the door. Cowboys, tourists and families crowded the streets. No one noticed her. Not one besotted stalker. She could do this. Another deep breath and she turned to lock the door.

As the lock clicked into place, a chill went up her spine. A presence behind her. She jumped, screamed and spun with her purse, ready to wallop.

Mitch held his hands up in surrender. "It's just me."

The shaking started and she couldn't stop it.

"Hey, you're okay." He gently took her in his arms.

The shaking didn't let up and, to top it off, she started crying.

"Give me your keys. Let's get you back inside."

"I don't think I got it locked and I'm pretty sure I dropped my keys."

"Here they are." He stooped to retrieve them, then gently turned her toward the door.

Once inside, he locked the door behind them, led her to the stool near the register and handed her a tissue. "Sit down. Deep breaths."

"I can't live like this."

"You're safe."

"I know. My head says I am. But my heart doesn't believe me."

"What were you doing outside by yourself anyway?"

"I'm twenty-eight years old." Her laugh came out sarcastic. "I ought to be able to go outside by myself. I thought it was time I walked over to Cowtown by myself."

"You've been through a harrowing ordeal. Just give yourself time."

"I used to go out for lunch." She dabbed the tissue under her eyes. Probably looking like a raccoon about now. "I used to come back here after the rodeo and do inventory. I used to have a life."

"And you will again."

"What happens in December when you go back on weekend duty?"

"I've already thought about that. Natalie and Lane—"

She let out a derisive chuckle. "My older sister shouldn't have to walk me to work."

"Okay, Bob would probably send Glen or someone else on the Cowtown payroll over."

"But he shouldn't have to. I ought to be able to cross the street by myself."

"Listen, Caitlyn, I know you don't realize it, but you've made amazing progress." His hands settled on her shoulders. "You walked the streets of San Antonio."

"With you."

"And if it were up to me, I'd spend the rest of my life escorting you around."

Sweet torment.

"But, I do have to go back to weekend duty for the month of December. And you do need to overcome your fears, but it hasn't quite been two months since your attack. Take it slow. You can't take something like this on by facing it head-on."

"So what? Do I need a shrink?"

"You need time. And maybe we could wean you. How about you head for Cowtown and I'll follow at a safe distance?"

Weaning herself from Mitch Warren. She'd already been through that once. And come December, he'd be gone. It hurt already.

She forced a smile. "Sounds like a start."

"After you, ma'am."

"I Will Survive" played from her purse and she dug out her cell. "Hello?"

"Caitlyn, it's Audra. How are you, dear?"

Her gaze flew to Mitch. "I'm fine. And you?"

"Wonderful. Listen, I'm planning our Thanksgiving dinner. All the kids, cousins, aunts and uncles are gathering at Grandpa's this year. I was hoping you might join us."

Including Mitch. She turned away from him. "That sounds great and it's very nice of you to invite me, but I'll be with my family for Thanksgiving."

"Is your family gathering on Thursday?"

"Actually, we can't get everyone together until Saturday."

"So spend Thanksgiving Day with us. Drive down on Wednesday and go to church with us that evening. Maybe even spend a few days with us there. Tara and Cody were so hoping you could come. And Mitch, of course."

Spend a few more days with Mitch. She swung back to face him. Her traitorous heart rocketed.

"I can't leave my store. Especially not on Black Friday."

"Caitlyn, dear, isn't taking off when you want the point of being the owner?"

She smiled. "It's supposed to be."

"Your employees can handle Black Friday. Please join us."

"I have to work the rodeo Friday and Saturday nights. Cowtown never takes holidays."

"Then return home Friday morning."

The following weekend, Mitch would be working and out of her life.

One final chance to spend time with him before they went their separate ways. One final time to say a last good-bye to his family. "I'd like that."

"Wonderful. We'll plan on seeing you, then."

Caitlyn hung up. "I guess you knew your mom planned to invite me for Thanksgiving?"

"She never mentioned it. Want to drive down with me? I'm leaving Wednesday morning."

Five hours stuck in a truck with Mitch. Her heart did a traitorous two-step. She shouldn't. Start weaning herself now. But she didn't want to wean herself at all.

"I have to be back by Friday night."

"Me, too." He grinned. "I have a certain rodeo queen I have to follow at a safe distance."

Her face heated. "You're coming back early for that?"

"A ranger keeps his promises. And I want to get some rest before I go back on duty. Since our schedules match, I don't see why I shouldn't escort a certain rodeo queen to Medina, too."

The word *no* simply wouldn't form. "Sounds like a plan."

"Great." His eyes lit up.

Eyes she could drown in. Arms she could happily die in. Why was she prolonging the agony?

Mitch spotted the exit. "I know it's not on your bucket list, but do you mind if we stop at Bass Pro?"

"Fine by me." Caitlyn yawned.

"I won't take long, I promise. I just want to see if they have anything new. For someone who doesn't fish or hunt, I can't seem to drive by without stopping."

"Shopping for your man cave?"

"My cabin." He grinned and took the exit.

"It's a man cave."

"I've actually been thinking about feminizing it. You know, in case I ever get married. Maybe you can make suggestions."

She clammed up at that. He glanced over in time to see pink rise in her cheeks.

Knowing it frustrated her to waste time circling the parking lot looking for a close space, he parked in the first open spot he found.

"Great. A chance to stretch my legs." She got out and lifted her arms in the air, stretching right then left.

Mitch had to look away. "Most women hate this place. There's a huge aquarium filled with gigantic catfish with a bench facing it. That's where the women usually go."

They strolled across the parking lot. "I might find something interesting."

"They have women's clothing, but that may not excite you since you own a whole storeful. And there's lots of dead animals on the walls."

"Can't wait." She chuckled.

It didn't interest her in the slightest. But it was one of the things he'd always loved about her. She wasn't one of those high-maintenance women always insisting on her own way and what she wanted to do. Caitlyn went along with the flow.

Except when it came to his job.

They reached the door and she noticed the animal tracks imprinted in the walkway. "That's cool. Deer?"

"And turkey." He pointed to the smaller set of tracks.

Her head tipped back as she took in the tangle of antlers above the entryway.

Mitch managed to open the door for her before she smacked into it. "You might want to watch where you're going. It's usually pretty crowded."

"I've never seen anything like it." Her gaze scanned the fireplace inside the entryway, the deer heads and fish mounted on the walls, the coyotes and raccoons perched on rocky outcrops. "So many dead animals."

"I can come back another time if you don't like it. I know you're not overly fond of hunting."

"No. It's fascinating—in a terrible sort of way."

He frowned. "You sure you're okay?"

"Fine."

"You might like this section." He pointed to housewares.

"This is where I got almost everything for the cabin. Here and Cabela's."

"This would be a great place to find guy gifts." She checked out the light-switch covers decorated with antlers and fishing lures.

"My whole family shops here for me. See anything to feminize my cabin?"

"The lavender camo pillows would do it." Caitlyn blushed and kept her gaze averted from his. "If your future wife likes camo, that is."

"Do you like camo?" He stepped directly in front of her.

# Chapter 11

"Depends on the man." Caitlyn swallowed hard and held Mitch's gaze. "And what he does for a living."

Before he could respond, she turned her back on him and stared at the wind chimes.

Mitch blew out a big breath. Would he never get anywhere with this stubborn woman? He rounded a display of deer-antler lamps, clocks and art. Counting to ten, he took several deep breaths and chose a clock. Frustration tamped down, he headed for the wind chimes.

But Caitlyn was gone.

Why had he left her? She was probably frightened in this huge store full of guns and people, and she didn't know her way around.

"Caitlyn?"

No answer. No sign of her. He rounded several more displays like a frantic parent searching for a lost child, then dug his cell out of his pocket and punched in her number. It rang and rang and rang.

With country music over the speakers, numerous conversations amongst the shoppers and the splash of several waterfalls, she'd never hear her phone.

Mitch scanned the checkout area and service desk. No Caitlyn. Where would she go? She wouldn't be interested in the clothing. Surely she wouldn't have gone downstairs by herself. He neared the railing and looked down.

There she was. In front of the aquarium as if she didn't have a care in the world. Mitch's breathing steadied. He'd imagined her alone, having a panic attack. Instead, she stood there mesmerized by the fish—oblivious to his presence or anyone else's. Progress.

As if she felt him watching, her gaze met his. He smiled and she smiled back. But her smile melted and she focused on the aquarium.

Mitch descended the curving wooden stairway and stopped at her side. "Do you realize what just happened here?"

"What?"

"You wandered off in a crowded store. A store you don't know your way around in."

"I thought I'd check out the aquarium, so I asked a man where it was."

"You spoke to a man you don't know. And you weren't afraid."

"I wasn't." She smiled, but again it melted. "But we're in San Antonio. I probably haven't been here enough for some nut to fixate on me yet."

"Yes, the Stockyards is where you feel threatened. But this is a step. Would you have spoken to a stranger or wandered off the last time we were in San Antonio?"

"No." Her smile stuck this time.

"That's good." He cupped her face in his hands. "I think you're on your way to a worry-free life."

"I hope so." She took a step back from him.

His hands fell to his sides.

"I've never seen such enormous catfish. What kind of bear is that?" She pointed to a faded brown stuffed bear standing at its full height, claws and teeth bared.

"It's a Kodiak. My folks used to take pictures of us kids with it every time we went to see Grandpa to measure how much we'd grown each year."

"Take my picture with it. Natalie will flip." She dug her camera out of her purse and handed it to him, then scurried over to the bear like a kid with no worries. The Caitlyn she used to be.

"Make me a copy?"

"Why?" She stood beside the bear as he adjusted the digital lens and captured the image.

"I want to remember the first day I saw you with no fear in your eyes."

She smiled. "Okay."

"Get between its claws, like it's attacking you."

Striking a terrified pose, Caitlyn acted out the scenario for the camera. But it was only for the picture. She was coming back.

If only she'd come back to him.

Daylight pricked at Caitlyn's consciousness. She snuggled deeper into the covers. Woodsy cologne. Mitch's cabin. Mitch's bed. She sat up straight.

She'd managed to escape Mitch, but had ended up spending the night in his cabin. In his bed.

With all his family home, including his aunt, uncle and cousin Clay, along with Rayna and their preschooler, Caitlyn had volunteered to stay in a hotel.

But everyone had laughed, then informed her the nearest rentable cabins were in the next town, twenty minutes away. And so she'd ended up in Mitch's cabin—in his bed, while Clay's family was in the cabin guest room.

Even after a hot shower last night, she'd been unable to relax and hadn't fallen asleep until the wee hours of the morning. With Mitch a good mile away at his grandfather's house, he was still too close.

The cabin was quiet. She crept out of bed and dressed quickly. Coffee. Coffee would work wonders. Hopefully. She needed a strong cup of courage to face Mitch again. Why, oh, why, oh, why had she come?

Because she loved him. And her traitorous heart couldn't pass up a chance to be with him. Even though they could never *really* be together.

She quietly opened the bedroom door and tiptoed toward the kitchen.

"Hey, want a cup?" Rayna sat at the table, coffee in hand.

"Exactly what I came for." Caitlyn poured a steaming cup and doctored it to a nice creamy tan shade, then settled across from Rayna.

"I'm so glad we have this chance to get better acquainted. I can't believe we both live in tiny Aubrey and had never met until the publicity campaign."

"Proof that it's a myth everyone in a small town knows everyone." Caitlyn sipped her coffee.

"Well, I'm a bit of a newcomer still, but you knew Clay and Mitch in school?"

"Yep."

"How long have you loved Mitch?"

Caitlyn gasped. "I—"

"Don't try to deny it." Rayna shot her a knowing grin. "Tara told me the whole story."

"Oh." What whole story? Their high school years, their recent forced reunion or all of it?

Despite his twisted position on the too-short couch, Mitch lay still, straining, waiting, hanging on Caitlyn's next words.

Nothing. She'd tried to deny she loved him, but the ever-astute Rayna had called her on it. But what did *oh* mean?

He'd snuck in last night after everyone was asleep. He knew Caitlyn wouldn't want him there, but he wanted to be near in case she needed a safety net.

But now he should make a noise, sit up, let them know he was there. Instead, he listened like some gossipmonger. He had to know how Caitlyn felt. And she certainly wouldn't tell him.

"You know—" Rayna's voice again "—when I met Clay, I was city through and through. Grew up in Dallas. Never even visited Fort Worth and I'd certainly never been to Aubrey."

"What about now?"

*Come on Rayna, work with me here, take the subject back to me. I need to know how she feels about me.*

"I don't know what I ever saw in the city."

"Funny how life changes up on you sometimes."

"Or how the right man can change everything." Rayna whistled. "I took one look at Clay and I was a goner."

"Y'all are probably one of those couples who met and got married within a matter of weeks."

"Hardly." Rayna chuckled. "I fought loving him with everything in me."

"Why?"

"One word. Bulls." Rayna's voice trembled.

Mitch grinned. He knew exactly where Rayna was going with this. *Thank You, Lord, for letting my cousin marry such a brilliant woman.*

"So Clay was still riding then?"

"Yes. Do you have any idea how dangerous that can be?"

"Actually, I do. But I've never known any of the wives."

"Well, number one, I'm terrified of bulls and, number two, I just knew one would kill Clay, and then where would I be?"

"So what did you do?" Caitlyn's question came out barely a whisper.

"I broke up with him and didn't see him for a while."

"But something brought you back together."

The furnace kicked on, making it harder to hear.

"His friend died in a rodeo accident."

"Mel Gentry?"

"Yes. And even though Mel died during a bronc ride, it proved in a very painful way I was right about rodeo being dangerous. But I couldn't stay away from Clay. I knew he was hurting and I wanted to be there for him."

Rayna paused. Probably sipping her coffee. "I only planned to get him through the funeral. Until a very wise soul—in the form of Clay's pastor—reminded me that God's got this. He's in control of life and death. Not some bull."

The women fell silent. Mitch's heart raced as he listened for footsteps. What if they came over to the living room area and discovered him eavesdropping?

"I finally realized that if Clay was a telephone operator and it was his time, the ceiling could fall in on him. And I came to the conclusion that, even apart, I worried about him."

The furnace turned off, allowing him to hear better, and Mitch relaxed.

"So I decided I'd rather worry about Clay up close and personal. If anything happened to him, I didn't want to look back and regret the time I could have spent with him."

*Are you listening, Caitlyn? Do you regret our years apart?*

"But Clay ended up quitting the rodeo for you. And you're living happily ever after."

"He didn't quit for me. By then, he was beginning to feel the bumps and bruises more and Mel's death kind of took the fire for rodeo out of him."

A chair scraped against the floor and something clattered in the sink. Probably finishing with their coffee. They'd discover him soon.

"But Clay continued to compete for several months after we married. I sat through countless more bull rides with frayed nerves before he managed to retire still in one piece."

"Has he ever regretted quitting?"

"No. He's content with the dude ranch and our family. We just found out we've got another baby coming, and Clay's getting inducted into the Texas Cowboy Hall of Fame Museum in January."

"That's wonderful. Congratulations on both counts." Silence for a few seconds. "But Mitch will never quit."

"Probably not, but just because he has a job in law enforcement doesn't mean he'll die on duty. He might outlive all of us. Look at Grandpa—he retired from ranger duty in perfect health. And besides, don't you want to spend whatever time you have with the man you love for whatever time *he* has?"

Say it, Caitlyn. Say yes. *Say you love me and want to be* with me.

Something hit the floor in the guest room, hard and fast. The door burst open and hurried footfalls headed straight for the couch. Mitch closed his eyes.

"Uncle Mitch is sweeping on the couch?" Kayla giggled. "And he looks like a pretzel."

Caitlyn gasped. Another chair scraped the kitchen floor and more footfalls coming his way.

He squinted his eyes open and stretched, then sat up and reached for his niece. "Morning, punkin'."

With a cute giggle, Kayla flung herself at him.

"Sorry she woke you." Rayna flashed a conspiratorial grin.

Not fooled for a minute. Was Caitlyn?

Shock and distress showed clearly in the strained lines

of her beautiful face. She was obviously wondering if he'd been asleep or heard the conversation.

Though she hadn't come out and said it, enough had been said for him to know she still loved him. He could work with that.

"What are you doing here?" Her voice cracked.

"I thought you might feel frightened. I wanted to be here, just in case."

"Kayla, will you go wake your sleepyhead daddy up?" Rayna scooped her squirming daughter out of Mitch's arms and set the little girl on the floor. "Mitch, why don't you get your kinked muscles stretched out with a little walk? And take Caitlyn with you."

"I don't need a walk." Caitlyn's protest came too fast.

"Nonsense. The day's about to go into high gear. We'll all gather at the ranch for breakfast, and then the men are on deep-fried-turkey duty while the other ladies there tackle the vegetable dishes. Caitlyn and I are in charge of desserts here at the cabin. Get some fresh air while you can."

Caitlyn didn't answer. Her gaze landed on the lavender camo throw pillows he'd had Cody pick up at Bass Pro. She looked at him, then back at the pillows, and at him again.

"I think I'll freshen up a bit before we go for breakfast." She scurried to his room and shut the door behind her.

Mental note—buy a longer couch. He stretched and stood, feeling every kink. "Rayna, you're a gem."

She shot him a good-natured wink. "You two belong together. I'll help it along any way I can."

"Thanks. I need all the help I can get with that one."

But would Caitlyn listen? Had Rayna's advice sunk in? *Dear Lord, if we're meant to be—help her to see it.*

Why did she have to be in love with his entire family? Caitlyn scanned the faces at the Thanksgiving table that evening. Grandpa, Mitch's parents, Cody, Tara and Jared, plus Rayna, Clay, their adorable Kayla and Clay's parents.

Church the night before and breakfast this morning had been like coming home.

But this wasn't her home. This wasn't her family. She was here to say goodbye. To all of them.

Her gaze caught on Mitch's. And stuck. Her heart yearned for him.

Just not his job. Her gaze dropped to her plate. "The turkey's great. I've never had deep-fried turkey before."

"Must have been a woman who came up with it." Audra grinned. "Makes the men feel manly and saves the women a lot of fuss so we can concentrate on the rest of the meal."

"Audra works magic in the kitchen." Wayne scooped a bite of pecan pie into his mouth and rolled his eyes with a moan.

"Actually, Tara and I did the veggies. Rayna and Caitlyn conjured up the desserts."

"Caitlyn's always been a great cook." Mitch's grin went straight through her heart.

"Amen." Wayne savored the last bite of his pie. "I'm thinking since the women worked hard while we swapped tales around the deep fryer, the men should pull cleanup duty."

"But the game's on." Cody's protest blended with several from the other men.

Audra patted Wayne's cheek. "Come on, ladies. Maybe there's something on TV besides football."

Caitlyn stood and fell in line behind the Warren women. Reprieve from the Mitch magnet.

A large hand caught hers. "We need to talk." Mitch's whisper sent shivers through her.

"You have cleanup duty."

"They've got it covered." He pulled her to the entryway,

slipped her rhinestone-lined denim jacket over her shoulders and reclaimed her hand. "Need a heavier jacket?"

"No, I'm fine." But she knew exactly what he wanted to talk about.

They stepped outside and Mitch led her down the steps to the path toward the river. The sun was still setting, but the moon already glowed bright.

"Did you like the pillows?"

"How did you pull that off?" She kept her gaze on the path. "You didn't buy them. I was with you."

"I had Cody pick them up on his way here."

"Oh."

"What does *oh* mean?" Mitch stopped in front of her and took her other hand in his.

"It means I hope your future wife likes them." Her eyes scalded.

"I was hoping—" Mitch tipped her chin up "—that would be you."

Everything in her wanted to say "me, too." If only he dug ditches for a living or pumped gas—anything other than law enforcement.

"I can't." Her gaze locked with his and her vision blurred.

"Just because your friend's dad died in the line of duty doesn't mean I will." He swallowed hard. "I still love you, Caitlyn. And I think you still love me."

"I do. But—" she shook her head "—you're going to get yourself killed, and I can't be around when that happens."

"Ten years, Caitlyn. I was a policeman for eight years and I've been a ranger for two. And I'm still here. In one piece."

"But for how long?"

"The death rate for rangers is very low. We're trained to handle any situation."

"I don't mean to bring up bad memories, but Tara told

me your partner died. And I assume he had the same training you had."

Mitch's gaze dropped to their hands. "He didn't die in the line of duty."

"What?"

"He was tired because his mom was fighting cancer. He was on his way home from visiting her in the hospital and fell asleep at the wheel. His death nearly killed me. I questioned myself for months—if I'd done anything differently, would Dylan have lived?"

"You can't blame yourself for a car accident."

"I knew he was tired." His jaw clenched. "I'd been at the hospital that day and I should have insisted he ride home with me. But I finally had to give it to God and trust it was Dylan's time to go home. I'll go when God wants me to— no matter what job I have. We all will."

The vise in her chest tightened at the mere thought of something happening to him. "I can't worry about whether you'll come home or not. I could never have children under those circumstances, and I want kids."

"And how's that working out for you?"

She jerked her hands out of his. "I'd rather be single and childless than marry a Texas Ranger."

"Then why? Why did you come here with me?"

"To say goodbye."

"Even though you love me? Even though I love you? We're meant to be together, Caitlyn."

The plea sent tremors through her heart, and she bolted toward the cabin.

"Caitlyn!"

But she didn't stop. Didn't answer.

All the way back to the cabin. She ran for his room, sank to the bed and covered her face with her hands, rocking back and forth.

A knock sounded on the door. She didn't answer.

"Caitlyn," Cody called. "Can I come in?"

"I'm okay." Her voice cracked.

"You sound like it. I saw you run by the house. Let me come in."

"It's open."

He stepped into the room and plopped down beside her, then patted his shoulder.

A watery laugh escaped as she laid her head on his shoulder.

"I take it the walk with Mitch didn't go well."

"Can I ride home with you instead? I know you're not going to Aubrey, but Natalie could meet us wherever is convenient."

"Sure. If you're sure that's what you want. I'm leaving for Waco Saturday morning. That's about halfway, but I can take you on home if you need me to."

She sighed and sat up. "Thanks. But I have to be home tomorrow night for the rodeo."

"I can leave early."

"Never mind." She rubbed her thumbs under her eyes. "Don't you ever get tired of the road?"

"Sort of."

"You could settle near Fort Worth and rodeo there without traveling."

"I've thought about it." Cody shrugged. "But what's the use of settling if I don't have anyone to settle with? Besides, traveling doubles my points, so I can get by with one rodeo per weekend instead of two. Fewer aches and pains that way."

"You're not seeing anyone?" She elbowed him in the ribs. "A handsome guy like you?"

"Just haven't met the right one. And from the looks of you, sometimes you meet the right one and it still doesn't work out."

Raccoon eyes. Again. Maybe she should switch to waterproof. "If he was the right one, it would work out."

"Probably won't see you again, will I?"

"Not unless—" she tried to summon a smile "—you settle in Aubrey or rodeo at the Stockyards."

"Well, you can't sit here and cry over my brother the rest of the evening. We're playing games, Grandpa's working on a puzzle. Come join us."

"I can't deal with Mitch. And I don't want to face your family. I shouldn't have come." She stood and paced the room. "I love them, you know. All of you. I always have. I thought I could come this last time and say goodbye. Without all this tension."

"I hate to leave you alone."

"I'm fine." She mustered up a wobbly smile. "You're a good friend, Cody."

"You know, just because you and Mitch can't work things out doesn't mean you have to be a stranger with the rest of us." He opened the door.

Mitch stood in the hall, his fist raised to knock. "I need to see Caitlyn."

"I love you, big brother. But I don't think she can take any more."

Great. Now she was causing problems between the brothers.

"I'm not here to upset her." His gaze caught hers. "I tried to find you another ride since I figure you're dreading five hours with me. But everybody else is staying until Sunday after church. So I'll take you home tomorrow as planned and I won't pressure you."

"Thanks." Her gaze flitted away.

"I want to make one stop in San Antonio, so we'll need to leave around nine o'clock to make sure you get home in time to unwind before the rodeo."

"I'll be ready."

But would she be? Ready to spend five hours in his truck with him? And then watch him walk out of her life? For good.

*Lord, give me strength.*

Mitch knew she was pretending to doze. Caitlyn had tearfully hugged each of his family members and waved goodbye as if she'd never see any of them again.

But he had one last trick up his sleeve. Would it work?

He took the exit, wound through the narrow downtown San Antonio streets and pulled into a parking garage. As he stopped at the booth to pay, she woke up.

"Where are we?"

"The Buckhorn Saloon. They have great food and a museum."

"But I'm not hungry after the breakfast Grandpa made."

"Neither am I. I want to show you something."

"I'm really not in the mood for any sightseeing."

"It won't take long."

"All right." She blew out a sigh.

His heart clenched. Why did being with him have to be such a chore for her? If he could only get her to stop being so stubborn.

She still loved him—she'd admitted it.

A smile broke out. He could work with that. If she'd let him.

*Lord, help me out here. Let her see what I see.*

Silence surrounded them as they made their way through the parking garage. Despite their footfalls and other people's conversations, the dead space between them was deafening. He longed to take her hand. But she didn't seem the slightest bit skittish. Except about him.

"You realize you're walking through a San Antonio parking garage and you're not afraid."

"I've been psyching myself up for you to be gone."

He swallowed hard. All the psyching in the world wouldn't prepare him for losing her again.

They emerged from the garage and moseyed down the sidewalk to the front of the historical saloon.

The huge longhorn statue above the entry and the antlers hanging over the door caught her attention.

"This is the gift shop." He opened the door for her. "Let me get our tickets. We can check this out later if we have time."

While he purchased the tickets, Caitlyn scanned the menagerie of deer, elk, bear and buffalo high above the restaurant area. "More dead animals?"

"Established in 1881, originally a bar. The owner loved antlers and horns, so when patrons couldn't pay, he accepted horns instead. His father made chairs and tables out of them. We'll see a few of them on the way to the museum."

"Museum?"

"The Texas Ranger Museum." He handed her a ticket.

Her fiery gaze met his. "So that's what this is about. You promised no pressure."

"None." He held his hands up in surrender then chanced touching the small of her back to urge her forward. "I just want to show you the museum."

Posture stiff, she jerked away. "Make it quick."

With a help-me glance toward the ceiling, Mitch followed.

A few buckhorn chairs lined the entryway. Antlers formed the legs, back and arms of each chair, with a rawhide seat.

"They look too dangerous to sit in."

At least the horns had snagged Caitlyn's curiosity enough for her to speak to him again.

Displays of the history of Texas Rangers and well-known officers along with their guns and newspaper accounts of heroism lined the museum. Caitlyn stopped to read several placards and Mitch read his favorites aloud.

"You remember hearing about the University of Texas tower sniper back in the sixties? One of the officers who stopped his reign of terror went on to be a Texas Ranger."

She turned away, seemingly unfazed and stopped at another display.

The urge to tell her about his new job teetered on the tip of his tongue. But no. What if he didn't like it? What if he ended up back on field duty? He couldn't marry her on desk duty and then go back to field duty.

And even if he could bring himself to leave the rangers for her, he could never guarantee her he'd be safe. If someone was in trouble, he'd always step in. That was who God had made him to be. She had to accept him and his job.

"Applicants have to have eight years of outstanding law enforcement service before they can apply to be rangers."

"I remember."

"Only 108 Texas Rangers have died in the line of duty. Most of those were in the Wild West days, and the rate has rapidly declined over the last several centuries."

"That makes 108 widows." Her chin wobbled. "And I don't want to be 109."

# *Chapter 12*

"Please try to see things from my perspective." Mitch cupped her cheek as a tear spilled, and he wiped it away with his thumb. "I need you to understand."

Her shoulders slumped. She took a step away from him and wiped at her eyes. "I'll try."

"Thank you." He took her hand in his and she didn't pull away as he showed her each display and recounted how Texas Rangers had stopped several crime sprees. She seemed to soften and her hand stayed in his.

"And finally, Bonnie and Clyde." He ushered her into the room detailing the infamous pair's crime spree. A bullet-riddled '34 Ford sat in the middle.

Caitlyn's hand flew to her chest. "Is that the actual car?"

"No. It's a replica."

"I don't want to see this." She closed her eyes. "Most of the people they killed were law enforcement."

"True. They were responsible for thirteen deaths, and nine of those murdered were law enforcement officers. But if Texas Rangers hadn't stopped them, think how many more innocent people would have died."

She opened her eyes and turned to face him. "I understand, Mitch. Texas Rangers have done a lot of good, stopped a lot of criminals. And I know how important being a ranger is to you—following your grandfather's legacy. It's noble and good, just like you." She pulled her hand out of his grasp and cupped his jaw. "But you've got ten years in now, the past two as a ranger. Couldn't they do it without you?"

A sucker punch to the gut. His shoulders slumped and a sigh escaped.

"I'll take that as a no." Her hand dropped to her side. "And because of that, we can never be. Just take me home." She headed for the exit.

He followed like a wounded puppy. *Is this it, Lord? This is how it ends. There's nothing else I can do.*

Other than try to get over Caitlyn Wentworth. Again.

Boisterous family chatter spilled from the dining room into the kitchen. Caitlyn had offered to get the pie for a reprieve. Acting happy was such a strain.

Even though she'd told Mitch that Lane would escort her to the rodeo now, she'd hoped Mitch would show up last night. But he hadn't.

It was probably all for the best. Mitch was a lot of things, but a quitter wasn't one of them. If he'd agreed to quit being a ranger for her, he'd have ended up resenting her.

Goo oozed up from under the pecans as she sliced the pie. Mouthwatering, but even her favorite holiday dishes and desserts didn't tempt her appetite.

Surrounded by her family at Thanksgiving, where she'd grown up, she should be genuinely happy.

Enough. Her family had worried enough about her. It was time to pull up her cowgirl boots and get on with it.

She took several deep, cleansing breaths, pasted on her best smile and picked up the pecan and pumpkin pies.

"Hey." Her cousin Jenna stepped into the room. "Need any help?"

"I think I've got it."

"You okay?"

"Fine."

"No." Jenna leaned her elbows on the island. "You're really not."

"I know Natalie told you all about me spending Thanksgiving with Mitch's family and you're both hoping it will work out between us. But it didn't. It won't."

"You sure?"

"Positive. I only went for closure. To say goodbye to him. And his family." Tears blurred her vision. "One final time."

"Hey, I didn't mean to upset you. Here, let me have the pies. You take a minute. But if you ever feel like talking, I'm here."

"Thanks." Caitlyn handed the pies over and swiped at her eyes. "I'll be back in a minute."

"I'll cover for you." With a dessert in each hand, Jenna hurried toward the dining room.

She and Jenna had always been close and had grown even closer when Natalie had been in her wild phase. Jenna always had her back.

The doorbell echoed through the house.

With a swipe under each eye, Caitlyn vaulted toward the door. Maybe with the distraction of an unexpected visitor, she could slip out and go for a walk to gather herself.

"I'll get it. Was anybody else coming?" She didn't slow as she entered the dining room.

Mama dropped her fork and it clattered against her plate. "Maybe that's Trent."

"I thought he wasn't coming." Daddy set his fork down.

"He appreciated the invite, but he did say no." Caitlyn

patted Mama's shoulder. "I don't think he's ready to re-unite with the family he never knew about, so don't get your hopes up, Mama."

Maybe telling her about the Millie connection hadn't been a good idea. Mama looked tired, as if she hadn't been sleeping. Caitlyn gave her a final pat and then continued to the front door.

Smile in place, she swung the door open. Trent. And an older version of herself standing behind him. Caitlyn's jaw dropped.

"Mom came home." Trent smiled, and an inner light glowed from him.

"I see," she squeaked. "Come in."

"I hope this is okay." Millie hesitated at the threshold. "Probably should have called, but I didn't know what to say."

"I—I can't believe you're really here." She clutched a hand to her racing heart. "I'm Caitlyn."

"Claire's daughter."

"The youngest. Mama never stopped missing you. She'll be thrilled, ecstatic, overwhelmed." All the years of Mama searching and longing and now Millie had shown up at their door. Through misty vision, Caitlyn ushered them toward the dining room. "Mama, there's someone here to see you."

Millie put a cautioning hand on Caitlyn's shoulder. "Don't you think we should prepare her first?"

"Trust me, she's been preparing for this moment for thirty years." She stepped into the dining room. All eyes turned her way. She motioned for Millie to enter.

Her aunt took a deep breath and stepped through the doorway.

Gasps echoed around the table, but Caitlyn focused on Mama.

"Millie?" Mama stood and banged into the food-laden table.

With tears steadily flowing, all Millie could do was nod.

"You're home." Mama pushed her chair back and launched herself at her sister.

The two sisters clung to each other as if they wanted to make up for thirty years of hugs. Through her own tears, Caitlyn scanned the faces around the table. Not a dry eye.

Thanks to Mitch.

The phone rang. Mitch sighed and let it ring. If it were duty related, it would be his cell, and there wasn't anyone he wanted to hear from. Except Caitlyn.

The machine clicked on. Silence while his muted greeting played, then the beep. "Mitch, it's Caitlyn."

Had she changed her mind? About letting him take her to the rodeo? About their future?

He vaulted toward the phone, whacking his shin on the coffee table. "Ouch. Hello."

"Ouch?"

"I bumped the coffee table." He rubbed his throbbing shin. "I'm glad you called."

Silence. "Um, I'm only calling because I wanted to tell you Aunt Millie is home."

His heart plummeted. She hadn't changed her mind. But at least her aunt was alive. "How is she?"

"Fine. She and Mama had a tearful reunion. Actually, we pretty much all did. Even Lane was blubbering. But don't tell him I told you that."

Mitch chuckled. "I won't. Did she say where she's been?"

"Texarkana—the Arkansas side. She saw his obituary, and that's what brought her home."

"Well, I'll be."

"Thank you. For bringing her home."

"I'm glad it worked." He settled on the couch. "Did she explain why she left?"

"She loved him." Caitlyn's tone echoed disbelief. "Initially. But she was only sixteen. After a few months, she got a glimpse of his dark side when he slapped her for talking to another guy. She tried to break up with him, but he threatened to kill her entire family if she didn't run away with him."

"Where did they run to?"

"Oklahoma. He got her a fake ID, made her go by Cammie and forced her to marry him."

Happy conversation echoed in the background. Apparently, the reunion was still going on.

"After Trent was born, Stuart became more aggressive. She didn't want Trent witnessing the violence as he got older, so she tried to leave—taking Trent with her." Caitlyn's voice cracked. "But Stuart caught up with her. He told her he'd always find her and if she ever tried to take Trent away from him again, he'd kill them both."

"So she left without him." He cleared his throat. "Probably hoping the violence would stop with her gone."

"Exactly. She decided she'd rather he kill her than live the way she and Trent were living, so she left. But that time, he didn't catch up with her. She'd watched him make fake IDs, so she tried her hand at it and started over in Texarkana."

"I guess she didn't see it in the newspaper when Stuart went to jail for beating Trent?"

"No. She missed it. But she always scanned the obits, hoping to see his name there so she could come home."

"I can understand why she wanted him dead." He closed his eyes, savoring the sound of the joy in her voice.

"Yeah. Anyway, once she saw the obit, she headed home, but it took her a few more days to get her courage up to try to find Trent. Hang on a second."

A child's voice sounded in the background, but he couldn't understand the words.

"I'll be back in a minute, sweet pea." Caitlyn paused.

He imagined her with their children.

"Sorry, Hannah's wondering where I got off to. Anyway, Millie was afraid Trent would hate her for leaving. And initially he was angry, but they talked it out and showed up at my parents' as we started our Thanksgiving dessert."

"That's awesome."

"Yeah, it really is." Her voice filled with wonder. "A Thanksgiving blessing."

If only there could be a blessing for him and Caitlyn.

"I told Millie about my ordeal and you reopening the case. We're all very grateful."

"I love happily ever afters." *I'd especially love one with you.* He cleared his throat. "I'll need to talk to her at some point. To wrap up the case. Maybe you could bring her to my office in Garland one day next week."

Silence echoed, until he wondered if she'd hung up. "Caitlyn?"

"I'll tell her. Mama and Daddy will probably bring her. Anyway, I wanted to fill you in. And thank you."

"Glad to be of service, ma'am."

"Um, goodbye, then."

Goodbye? Not so long or see ya later. But goodbye.

He swallowed the knot lodged in his throat. "Goodbye, Caitlyn."

Despite all his efforts, all his dreams, all his longing, he had to let her go. Again.

As soft strains of "Just as I Am" filled the sanctuary, Caitlyn knelt at the altar. Life hurt. Everything hurt, including attending church. Even though Millie and Trent had come for services.

Home. Her church home. Her aunt was home. She had a new cousin. Her spirits should lift.

But all she'd thought about during Sunday-school class and service was Mitch. And never seeing him again.

*Oh, Lord, why did he have to come back into my life?*

To keep her safe. But now he was gone. Back on weekend duty. Risking his life to keep other people safe.

Her hose-clad knees ached from kneeling at the unyielding wooden altar. *Help me forget him and concentrate on returning to normal.*

Normal. *What is that, Lord? I can't even park behind my store anymore without almost having a panic attack.*

*Lord, give me strength to forget Mitch. Help me not to love him. Help me to feel safe without him. And happy.*

Happy? Had she ever been happy since he'd walked away ten years ago?

"'But let all those that put their trust in thee rejoice: let them ever shout for joy, because thou defendest them: let them also that love thy name be joyful in thee.' Psalm 5:11," the pastor quoted. "Are you burdened? Come lay your burdens at the feet of Jesus. Leave this place shouting for joy."

She didn't need Mitch to be happy. She needed to find her happiness in the Lord.

How long had it been since she'd shouted for joy? Thou defendest them. *Thou defendest me.*

A lightness filled her chest.

*You've got this, God. You'll never forsake me. When Stuart Stevens attacked me, You were there giving me strength to fight. To escape.*

*And if I'd been tortured, You'd have been there to give me strength to endure. If it had been my time to die, You'd have been there to carry me home.*

The heavy burden slipped off her shoulders. She had no reason to fear. "You've got this, Lord," she whispered. "Thanks for the reminder."

As she stood and walked back to her seat, she couldn't stop smiling. For the first time in months.

A sense of accomplishment lightened Caitlyn's spirit even more as she parked behind her store. Head held high, she strolled to the back door and unlocked it without running or looking over her shoulder.

Inside, she leaned against the wall. "Thank You, Lord."

She buzzed through opening chores—turned all the lights on, emptied the trash and stocked the register.

The Christmas decorations were up, but it needed something more. A quick scan of the closet and she found two strands of multicolored bulbs. She grabbed a pair of her bestselling men's boots out of the stockroom.

The supple black shaft with white-stitched wings surrounding a cross reminded her of Mitch's recommitment to Christ. She propped the boots in the window, wrapped a strand of lights all around them and plugged the lights in. Then stood back, tilting her head to the side. Cute.

Cute enough that she grabbed a women's pair, repeated the process and set them in the opposite window. Satisfied, she took the empty boxes out to the back Dumpster and returned to the stockroom. She pulled out a box containing his size, opened the lid and the scent of leather filled her senses. Probably a little flashy for everyday, but perfect for church.

Maybe she'd ship them to him for Christmas.

She stashed the boots in the closet and dug new trash bags out. The broom in the closet caught her eye. She grabbed it, unlocked the front door and took a deep breath. One foot over the threshold. Then two.

The brick-lined streets never filled this early. Truth be told, it was too early for her. But she had to fight her night-owl tendencies daily to run a business.

Birds chirped from the trees. A brisk wind whipped

down the streets with only a few workers and tourists strolling along. She didn't scan the faces, didn't zone in on the men. Instead, she swept the sidewalk. With each swipe, she relaxed more, and she even swept the walk in front of the Texas Cowboy Hall of Fame Museum next to her store and the gift shop on the other side of hers. Her broom met up with a cowboy boot.

"Oh, I'm sorry." She looked up.

Keith, a clerk from the gift shop next door. *Please don't ask me out again.*

"Hey, Caitlyn." He adjusted his cowboy hat. "Long time, no see."

"I've been really busy."

"I noticed. I've only seen you scurrying back and forth across the street. With your sister. Or that guy." The unspoken question rang clear in his tone.

"Well, I've decided to get out more." She propped her chin on the broom handle.

"Is he your boyfriend?"

It was tempting to say yes to head him off. "No," she croaked.

"Good." He smiled. "In that case, how about having dinner with me Friday night?"

He was a nice guy, a good-looking guy, even. She'd never really noticed—light brown eyes and hair. It was tempting to go out to dinner and get on with her life. But she wasn't interested in him. In anyone other than Mitch. And she couldn't use this nice guy to try to forget Mitch.

"I work Friday nights."

"Oh, yeah, I knew that. It could be a weeknight."

"It's a nice offer, Keith, and you're a really nice guy—"

"But… I hear a but coming."

"It's not a good time for me."

A disappointed sigh escaped him. "Well, if you find a good time, let me know."

"You should probably ask somebody else. I'm sort of nursing a broken heart." For the past ten years. But he didn't need to know that.

"Well, whoever it was that let you get away must be crazy."

"Thanks." Her heart warmed at the compliment. "Um, I'd better get back inside and finish up."

"Caitlyn," Natalie called from in front of the museum. "What are you doing outside—flirting with a cute cowboy?"

Caitlyn's face heated. "Keith, this is my sister, Natalie. She's happily married, thinks everyone else should be and is known for saying whatever she thinks—even when she thinks wrong."

"Nice meeting you, Natalie. Trust me, she wasn't flirting, but I was." With a parting wink, Keith turned and went inside the gift shop.

"Why are you outside? And why weren't you flirting with him?"

"I'm outside because I had a good talk with God at church yesterday and He reminded me He's in control. Not some stalker. I even parked in the back lot today."

"Wow. You seem…"

"Free."

"I'm so glad. Mitch wanted me to check on you this morning, so I'll have good news to report."

Her heart twisted. "Why is he checking on me?"

"He's worried about you. Like we've all been."

"You can officially tell him and everyone else I'm fine. I'm no longer cringing at the sight of my own shadow."

"It looks good on you." Natalie hugged her. "You look and sound like your old self. And so, since you're feeling better and you're determined Mitch isn't the one, why not cowboy Keith?"

"I'm not interested. In anyone right now. I just want to

enjoy my life again. Without you, or anybody else, trying to fix it for me. I'm fine."

"We want you to be happy."

"I know. And I love you for it. But I don't have to have a man to be happy. I am happy."

But her words held a hollow ring. As hollow as her heart.

"All right, I'll see you tomorrow, probably. And Lane and I will be here Friday to walk you over to the rodeo."

"Tomorrow I'm going to check on the Dallas store. And Friday—thanks, but I'll walk myself to the rodeo."

Natalie smiled and gave her another squeeze. "Glad to have you back."

Now if she could just move on. Without Mitch.


"I don't understand." Raquel squinted up at Mitch in the dim lighting as they made slow progress around the Galleria ice rink. "If she loves you and you love her, why aren't you together?"

"It's not that simple." He watched Hunter glide across the ice. If only Dylan could be here to watch his son grow.

"Did you tell her about your transfer?"

"No."

"Because?" Her left eyebrow lifted.

"I don't know that I'll be a forensic artist for the rest of my life. What if I stink at it? What if I get bored with it? If Caitlyn can't accept me with whatever job I have, we don't have a future."

"It's a lot to accept. Trust me." Raquel pulled her jacket tighter.

Offering comfort, he took her hand in his. "You know more than anybody."

"I miss him so much. Sometimes Hunter is a comfort— I mean, he looks exactly like Dylan. Acts just like Dylan. But sometimes looking at him hurts. He's so much like his father that I miss Dylan even more."

"I'm sorry."

"Don't go blaming yourself again." She elbowed him in the ribs. "I like this new right-with-God-and-myself Mitch."

"I'm not blaming myself. I miss him, too. And I'm sorry he's gone. For you, for Hunter and for me."

A small boy careened toward Hunter. Mitch winced, expecting a crash, but the child righted himself and skated away.

"You need to stop spending so much time with us. You're off duty today and you're skating with us. You should be pursuing Caitlyn. Or someone else."

"I love my time with y'all. But what you said goes both ways, you know. How long's it been since you've been on a date?"

"It's different." She looked away. "And you know it."

"But I also know Dylan would want you to be happy."

"Maybe I can't be happy with anyone but Dylan."

"You'll never know if you don't at least consider letting someone else into that empty heart of yours."

"My heart is quite full, thank you very much. So full there's no room for romance."

Maybe she could only be happy with Dylan. A car accident had ripped that happiness away. Maybe Mitch could only be happy with Caitlyn. And his choice of career had ripped away his only chance of happiness.

No. They'd both trust in the Lord for happiness, no matter what happened in the future.


Freedom. Caitlyn had forgotten what it was like to go wherever she wanted. Without fear. *Thank You, Lord.*

Garlic, deep-fried batter and onions. The Galleria food court teemed with people. She stopped at the rail and looked down on the skaters. One of these days, she needed to take time to do that. It had been years since she'd ice-skated.

A teenage girl sailed across the ice and spun up in the

air like an Olympian. Caitlyn held her breath until the girl landed. Still upright.

Children barely big enough to walk clambered around the rink holding their parents' hands. Couples held hands as they glided around and around.

Back when she and Mitch were dating, they'd come here several times. She closed her eyes—lost in memories. The warmth of his hand on hers. His strong arms around her when she stumbled. In fact, she'd stumbled a few times on purpose. Their first date, their first kiss, the first time he'd said he loved her.

*Stop it, Caitlyn. It's over.*

She opened her eyes and focused on a couple. The man's muscular build, height and dark hair reminded her of Mitch. She turned her attention to the slender blonde at his side instead. The woman stumbled, her lips parted in a gasp. The man caught her in his arms and dipped her dramatically. They laughed as he helped her up, and a little boy came running to join them.

The man picked the little boy up and spun him round and round. The child giggled and the man's head tilted back as he chuckled.

And for the first time, Caitlyn got a good look at his face. Mitch.

Her heart crashed.

# Chapter 13

Caitlyn spun away from the rink and bolted for her store. Be happy for him. He was moving on. And he had every right to be happy. Without her.

The window display of her store glowed with lights, sparkly bows and festive wreaths, offering sanctuary.

One of the clerks glanced up from helping a customer. "Your cousin called looking for you. He sounded young. I didn't know you had any young cousins."

*Neither did I, until my life exploded.* "Thanks, I'll go call him back now."

Her manager frowned at her as she headed for the back of the store to her office.

The manager and both clerks were busy helping customers while several more browsed. She should help someone, but on the verge of a meltdown, she didn't have it in her at the moment.

She sank into the chair at her desk. Something else to

think about. Anything. She pulled out her cell and punched Trent's number.

"Hey, you rang?"

"I did it." Excitement echoed in his tone.

"Did what?"

"Asked my girlfriend, Faith, to marry me."

Caitlyn smiled. Young love. Nothing like it. "And she said yes?"

"Definitely."

"What about her dad?"

"I visited with her family on Thanksgiving Day. We had a long talk and he gave me his blessing to ask her. I was planning on asking at Christmas, but I couldn't wait."

"You're staying in college, though, right?"

"Definitely. I've finished my first year and I'm working part-time at a veterinary clinic."

"I'm really happy for you, Trent. Really."

"Me, too. So the wedding is on New Year's Eve at the Ever After Chapel."

Her heart stuttered. Where Mitch had proposed.

"That soon? That's only three weeks away."

"I know. It's crazy. But we're not having a huge wedding or anything. We both want it to be simple. All her family lives here. And we don't want to wait any longer. We've dated almost a year."

"Sounds like you've got it all worked out. Congratulations."

"We'll be sending an invitation to the fam. I hope y'all can come."

"We wouldn't miss it."

"You wouldn't happen to know Mitch's address, would you?"

The air went out of her lungs. She closed her eyes. Another run-in with him at her cousin's wedding. Would he bring his someone new? "Just send his invitation to the Texas Ranger headquarters in Garland."

"Duh. Why didn't I think of that? I gotta go. I've got a class in a little bit, but I wanted to tell you the news since you encouraged me not to give up on Faith."

"I'm really glad. And I'll see you on New Year's Eve if not before." Caitlyn ended the call and pressed her fingers against the slight throb in her temple. She had to get out of here.

She gathered her purse and briefcase. As she hurried through the store, her manager sent her a silent SOS. Even more customers were browsing.

"Can I help someone?" Caitlyn stashed her things under the counter and approached a woman in the hat section.

Surely the store would slow enough for her to escape back to Fort Worth soon.

Before she ran into Mitch and his someone new.

The day before Christmas Eve and the store had hopped all morning before slacking off at lunch. Did no one shop ahead anymore?

"What size did you need again, ma'am?" Caitlyn couldn't seem to focus.

"Eight."

Caitlyn dug through the stack of jeans with blingy back pockets. The woman looked more like a twelve, but she'd go along with the fantasy.

"Here you go. Just let me know if you need something smaller and I'll bring them to the dressing room."

"Thanks." The woman beamed as she headed for the dressing room.

"Smaller?" Natalie whispered. "You're a genius."

"When she asks for a ten and then a twelve, I'll tell her how this brand is cut really small." Caitlyn shrugged. "I figure my job is to make people feel good about themselves."

"Leave it to you to find a noble cause in selling clothes." Natalie grinned. "So are you going to Trent's wedding?"

Caitlyn blew out a sigh. "Yes."

"What's wrong?"

"He's inviting Mitch, too. And I'm afraid Mitch will bring his girlfriend."

Natalie's eyes went wide. "Mitch has a girlfriend? You're crazy. The only one he's ever noticed is you."

"I saw them." Her voice cracked. "At the Galleria ice rink."

"Maybe they're just friends."

"They looked awfully cozy. And there was a little boy with them." Like a ready-made family.

"Hmm." Natalie tapped her chin with an index finger. "I know—invite cowboy Keith to the wedding. That way if Mitch isn't alone, you won't be, either."

"No. Absolutely not. I'd rather face Mitch and his girlfriend and leave as soon as the wedding is over."

"Suit yourself." Natalie shrugged. Her cell rang and she dug it out of her pocket. "Hey, handsome."

"Ms. Wentworth," the lady in the dressing room called.

"Yes." Caitlyn scurried to her door.

"These seem a little small. I don't know what the problem is—I always wear an eight."

"This line is cut small. Let me get you the next size." She scooped up the ten she already had waiting at the counter, took them to the customer and dug out a size twelve.

"Caitlyn, get your purse. We need to go." The usually soft lines of Natalie's face showed strain.

Her heart jolted. "What's wrong?" Please not Mama or Daddy. "Can I finish with my customer?"

"Jennifer's back from lunch." Natalie gestured to her clerk.

"I'll take over." Jennifer shot her a tense smile. "You go."

"Tell me what's wrong." Caitlyn's gaze locked on her sister.

"That was Lane.... He had the radio on. I'm sure it's not Mitch, but—"

Shock waves went off in her chest. "What about Mitch?"

"Something about a robbery and a shoot-out with a couple of Texas Rangers. It's probably not Mitch, but I thought I'd take you home and we could—"

"Garland. Take me to headquarters in Garland."

"Of course." Natalie shoved Caitlyn's purse at her.

"Um, the customer might need these twelves." Caitlyn's voice quivered.

"I know the drill—the line is cut small. Go." Jennifer smiled again.

"I'm sure Mitch is fine." Natalie opened the door for her. "But you won't be until you know for sure."

Mitch followed the forensic artist's instructions. He should have been in Rockwall, rounding up the robbery suspect. Maybe if he'd been there, no one would have gotten hurt. At least it was a clean shoulder wound. But the suspect had gotten away and Mitch itched to be in on the hunt.

Instead, he sat in a quiet office glued to a computer screen.

"Very good. You're a natural." George smiled. "With your artistic skills, I can retire knowing you've got this department under control."

"I'm not as good as you."

"I've only got thirty-seven years on you."

"No pressure." Mitch grinned and saved the age progression on a missing person's case they'd updated.

The office door opened and a frantic-looking Timmons stepped in. "Sorry to interrupt your training, but there are two women here to see you and they're causing a disruption."

"Who?" Mitch frowned.

"One of them is Ms. Wentworth."

Mitch's heart did a flip.

"I believe the other lady said she's her sister."

"Ma'am, y'all can't be in this area." A harried clerk sounded near his office. "I told you to stay in the lobby."

"We're not leaving." Natalie's voice came from the hall. "Not until my sister sees Mitch Warren. I don't care if you arrest us both."

Mitch stood and bolted for the doorway. "They're with me."

"Here he is, Caitlyn," Natalie said. "He's right here."

A sob escaped Caitlyn. Her eyes were red, cheeks tearstained.

Had something terrible happened to their parents? Mitch hurried to her and drew her into his arms. "What's wrong? What's happened?"

"We heard the news." Natalie wiped at a stray tear. "She was worried it was you in the shoot-out."

The tears were for him. Tangible proof she loved him.

Mitch walked her to his office and closed the door. Everyone had disappeared without him even noticing, leaving them alone.

"I'm fine." He ran his hand down the length of her soft waves. "I'm fine."

"I thought you might die."

"I've been right here all day."

The shaking stopped. Her sobs quieted. She pulled away from him and swabbed her face. "I'm glad. Really glad. Did anyone get hurt today?"

"Salvo—remember him from guard duty when you

were in the hospital? He took a shot in the shoulder, but he'll be fine."

"Good." She turned toward the door.

"You're leaving?" He grabbed her by both shoulders.

"Yes."

Gently, he turned her to face him. "You can't."

"I have to."

"You just took ten years off your life worrying and sobbing because you thought I might be hurt and now you're going to walk out on us. Again?"

Her watery eyes looked into his soul. "How many tens of years do I have to give?"

"Caitlyn, we love each other. And obviously you're going to worry about me whether we're together or not."

"I shouldn't have come here." She backed away from him. "But I couldn't seem to stay away. I had to know if you were all right and I'm so thankful that you are. But there's no future for us. And besides—" her voice cracked "—you're seeing someone else."

Someone else? He frowned. "No. I told you, I'm not seeing anyone."

"I saw you with her."

"There's no her."

"I was at the Galleria checking on my store."

The Galleria? Oh. The ice rink.

"That was Raquel. My partner's widow. She's the friend I told you about. We're friends—that's all."

"Y'all seemed awfully cozy."

"Friends, Caitlyn. We grieved over Dylan together. I try to spend time with her son, but that's all. There's never been anyone but you."

"You should focus on Raquel." Caitlyn shook her head. "She understands the life of a ranger's wife. You could move on with her, and her son needs a father."

"I don't love her and she doesn't love me. I want to move on with you."

"I can't." Her face crumpled and she covered it with both hands.

He reached for her.

"Don't." She took another step back. "Just let me go. And please—" she swiped at her tears and took a deep breath "—don't follow me." She turned and rushed out the door.

He couldn't just let her go. He ran after her, but she was already halfway to the lobby. His phone rang.

Still on duty. Mitch stopped. Everything in him wanted to let it ring. Instead, he hurried back to his office. "Warren here."

"It's Timmons. I hope you've got your situation under control. We need you down at the hospital to get Salvo's description of the shooter."

"On my way." Mitch closed his eyes.

The hair at Caitlyn's temple was tear soaked. Her sinuses were so swollen she couldn't breathe. She rolled over.

Heavy raw ash furnishings complemented the horses of various colors stampeding across her sage comforter. The Texas lone star was carved in her headboard, the mirror on the dresser and top drawer of the chest. Her favorite room in the house—her sanctuary.

The matching glass display case Mama and Daddy had had custom-made for her birthday held all her barrel-racing trophies, belt buckles and several crowns from her rodeo-queen competitions.

But even her favorite room was no comfort.

Her phone rang beside the bed. Probably Natalie checking on her again. And her persistent sister would keep calling until she answered.

"I'm okay."

"I'm glad." Cody laughed. "I'm okay, too."

"Oh, I thought you were Natalie. She's worried about me."

"Do tell."

"Long story." She sat up and adjusted the covers around her. "How are you?"

"Good, but I need a huge favor. I have a blind date on New Year's Eve and I need you to be there."

"My cousin is getting married that night. I have to go to the wedding." And face Mitch again.

"Our date is over lunch."

"Why do you want me to crash your date?"

"So I won't be nervous."

"Don't you think your date will think it's strange for you to bring another woman on your date?" She swabbed her face with a tissue and hoped she didn't sound like she'd been crying.

"We're both trying to keep it real casual." He sighed. "That's why we set it up for lunch. And she's bringing a friend, too."

"This is sounding like a very crowded date. What are you doing going on a blind date, anyway? You're a nice, cute guy. Women should fall at your feet."

"Thank you, thank you very much."

His Elvis impression needed work, but it tugged a laugh out of her. Cody was probably the only one who could do that today.

"But until someone falls at my feet, a mutual friend set me up on this date and I'm nervous about it. *Please.*"

"Where?"

"You don't even have to travel far. Moms on Main at noon."

"Oh, all right." She rolled her eyes. "But just this once."

"You're my all-time bestie."

"You owe me."

Cody deserved happiness, and if she could help him meet someone, she'd gladly do it. Maybe his effervescence and sense of carefree fun would keep her tension down since she'd have to face Mitch at the wedding that evening.

For the last time.

No matter what she heard on the news, after Trent's wedding, she would do her best to avoid Mitch.

And he would not ruin Christmas tomorrow. She would focus on celebrating her Savior's birth. Her Mitch addiction paled in comparison.

Determined to pull herself together again, she threw the covers back.

The mirror told no lies. Swollen, puffy eyelids. She dressed quickly and took a little extra time with her makeup, hoping to cover up the evidence. But it was no use; she looked like she'd cried all night. Oh, well, she'd spend her day at the store. Last-minute shoppers would sidetrack her and by tomorrow, she'd be fine.

She hurried downstairs, slipped on her coat and went to check the mailbox. A shirt-box-size package and cluster of envelopes bound together with a rubber band rested against a pillar by the steps. Several bills, junk mail, last-minute sale ads and the box—return address Garland.

Her breath froze in her lungs. Had he gotten his boots and felt he should send her something in return? She checked the mailing date on the package. Mailed the same day she'd sent his boots.

Stepping inside, she pulled the end of the box open and poured the contents out on the coffee table. A puzzle—exactly like the one she'd helped Grandpa with—a navy jewelry box and a note.

With shaking hands, she flipped open the lid of the velvety box. A pair of sparkling sapphire earrings. With blurred vision, she opened the note.

Dear Caitlyn,
They reminded me of your eyes. Be happy.
Love always,
Mitch

Yes, she would always love him. She released a tremulous breath. So much for pulling herself together. Again.

Moms on Main was hopping, as usual. Caitlyn scanned the crowded restaurant and it took her a while to spot Cody at a booth near the register. He stood and hurried to meet her.

Her curious gaze lingered on the booth. The back of a man's head. Dark hair. Mitch. Her breath stalled. The woman from the mall, Raquel, sat across from him beside where Cody had been seated.

"Hey, you made it."

"You didn't tell me—"

"Because you wouldn't have come. He's been wanting me to meet Raquel for a while."

Her hand went to an earring. She'd have never worn them if she'd known he'd be here. "I'm leaving."

"He knows you're here. What will he think if you leave?"

"I don't care." She shot him a glare. "You set me up."

"Y'all are crazy about each other and I love you both. What good would I be as a brother and friend if I stood idly by while you're both miserable?"

"A sweet sentiment. But I'm not miserable and I'm leaving."

"You are miserable. And Mitch told me he's going to the wedding, too. You've probably been dreading it since the moment you learned your cousin invited him."

The protest danced on the tip of her tongue. But Cody knew her too well. Her mouth clamped shut.

"So stay for lunch. Get facing Mitch over with and you'll be able to enjoy your cousin's wedding."

Behind Cody, she saw Mitch stand and Raquel did, too. Both headed in their direction. Too late to scurry away with her tail between her legs.

"Caitlyn, meet Raquel. I've wanted y'all to meet for a while."

Raquel offered her hand. "You're just as beautiful as Mitch described."

Heat crept up her face. "Thanks. He never told me much about—" Insert foot in mouth.

"Every time I talk about Raquel very much—" Mitch shrugged "—people think we're an item."

"And Mitch has been in love with you ever since I've known him." Raquel smiled. "So he certainly wouldn't take the chance of you thinking anything was going on with us."

For once, Mitch was speechless, as Caitlyn's face singed.

"I'm glad." Cody cleared his throat. "They're not an item—I mean. If y'all don't mind, Raquel and I will go back to the table."

"I think I'll leave, but it was nice meeting you, Raquel."

"I hope you'll stay, but if not I hope to see you again soon—with Mitch." Raquel shot him a conspiratorial smile.

"Don't be mad at me." Cody hugged Caitlyn, then followed Raquel back to the booth.

"They seem to have hit it off." Mitch's gaze never left hers. "I've been trying to introduce them. I don't know why God felt the need to surround me with stubborn people."

That stubborn zinger was meant for her. Caitlyn headed for the door.

Just outside, she heard footfalls behind her.

"Caitlyn, wait."

Mitch. Of course.

At least Caitlyn stopped, but she didn't turn to face him.

He grasped her shoulders and felt her shiver as he turned her around.

An approaching train blew its hollow, mournful whistle, sounding sadder than it ever had.

With a hard swallow, she focused somewhere near the top button of his shirt.

"I knew the earrings would be great with your eyes." He pushed her hair aside to see them. "Eyes I've never been able to forget. Thanks for the boots."

Her throat convulsed. "I thought since you saved my life and brought my aunt home, a new pair of boots was the least I could do. They reminded me of your recommitment to Christ. I love the earrings, but you really shouldn't have."

"Raquel's right, you know. I've loved you since before she ever knew me."

"Please don't."

The train trundled past and he waited until the noise quieted with a final blast of the lonely whistle.

"I believe God creates people for each other. He made us for each other, Caitlyn. Why else would we still love each other after ten years apart?"

"If we're created for each other—" her voice quivered "—why would He set up an obstacle we can't overcome?"

"Because, we can overcome it. All things are possible with God on our side. He's got it all in the palm of His hand."

Eyes brimming, she shook her head.

"What time are you going to the wedding tonight?"

"Five-thirty." Confusion pulled her brows into a frown.

"Mama, Nat and I are helping with last-minute details, so we have to be there early."

"Meet me at the Ever After Chapel."

Her breath caught.

The exact same thing he'd said to her ten years ago. The exact same place he'd proposed to her ten years ago. She obviously understood his intent.

"I'll be there anyway. For the wedding."

"I'll be under the big tree at six-thirty. Meet me there."

"And if I…can't?"

"I won't bother you again." His words came out barely a whisper. "It's up to you."

*Please let her be there, Lord.*

Willing his legs not to buckle, he turned away and went back into the restaurant.


6:28 p.m. Caitlyn released a long breath. In two minutes the man she'd loved since she could remember would be outside with a proposal. His second proposal. And she wouldn't be there.

Breathe. In and out. She scanned the whitewashed walls, simple walnut pews and pale hardwood floors of the chapel.

She'd never marry Mitch. Here or anywhere else. She had to get that through her head.

If she could remain upright and make it through this wedding, then Mitch would leave her alone. She wouldn't have to see him again. She could reclaim her Mitchless, prestalker life.

"Hey." Trent stepped inside the empty sanctuary. "Mitch is looking for you outside."

Emptiness gripped her. Light-headed and airy. Just stay upright.

"You okay?" He tucked her hand in the crook of his elbow.

"Fine. I never got around to eating lunch today." She pressed her free hand to her middle. "What were you doing outside, trying to peek through the windows and get a glimpse of your bride?"

"Actually, I was thinking about a cigarette." He shot her a sheepish grin. "I used to smoke several years ago. It tempts me every once in a while when I'm nervous. Have you seen Faith?"

"Yes, and she's beautiful. But I can't let you see her before the wedding." She wagged a finger at him. "So don't even try."

"I don't believe in superstitions. Not anymore."

"Me, neither. Actually, I never did. So what have you got to be nervous about?"

"I don't have a clue." His grin turned sappy. "I'm about to marry the girl of my dreams. Until death do us part. I'm great with that plan."

"I'm glad."

"Is Faith nervous?"

"Maybe about tripping down the aisle and getting her vows right, but not about you."

"Maybe that's why I'm nervous. I don't want to mess this up."

"You'll be fine." She patted his arm.

"You'd better go see about Mitch."

"He can wait." Her voice cracked. "I'd better go see if I can help the ladies."

She hurried toward the dressing room. If only she could pledge herself to Mitch—until death did they part. And trust him to live.

*Trust God.*

The thought came to her clear as day. And hit her in the gut with such force she had to stop walking and clutch the rawhide couch in the reception area for support.

God's got this. He's in control. Of Mitch's safety. Of

Mitch's life and death. She had to give God control of Mitch's safety, just as she'd given over control of her own. And trust God to see her through if anything happened to him.

6:31 p.m. She pressed a hand to her midsection and ran for the exit.

What if he'd already given up? What if he'd left?

Just inside the door, she stopped. He had to be there. He had to. With a deep breath, she stepped outside. Several guests arrived in a steady stream. She looked to her left.

No Mitch.

As her heart crashed to her toes, she ran down the steps and veered toward the parking area. He couldn't have gone far. She had to find him and explain.

*Please, Lord, don't let it be too late.*

"Caitlyn—the other big tree."

Her feet stalled and she spun around. Mitch stood under the large tree to the right of the entrance.

Tears blinded her and she launched herself into him, not caring who saw.

"Whoa, girl, don't take me down."

She kissed him with ten years of urgency, longing and despair.

A whistle reached into her brain, followed by applause and catcalls. People were watching. She pulled away.

Mitch swallowed hard. "Wow."

"Is that all you have to say?" She slid her hands up his shoulders and around his neck.

"No." He pulled free. "But I need to be able to think and I need to know where the change of heart comes from. I didn't really think you'd come."

"I realized God's got this. He'll see us through whatever our future holds." She moved closer.

He grinned and took a step back. "There's one more thing I need to tell you."

"What?"

"I took a transfer. I'm a forensic artist now. I sketch witnesses' descriptions of suspects, age-enhance missing persons' pictures and that sort of thing."

"You're not on the street anymore?"

"Nope. In an office—behind a desk."

She slugged him in the shoulder.

"Ow."

"Why didn't you tell me?"

"Because I wanted you to accept me, no matter what. And I start tomorrow. It may not work out."

"Why?"

"The other day when that shoot-out was going on in Garland, I was champing at the bit, feeling like I should have been there. I can't promise you I'll never go back to the field."

"Why did you take the transfer, then? I don't want you to end up resenting me."

"Actually, I put in for the transfer before we reconnected. I'm tired of holding people's lives in my hands. Too much stress. But I'm not sure I can be at ease out of the line of fire." He took a step toward her. "Can you live with that?"

"With God's help, I can." She closed the gap between them and wound her arms around his neck again. "And I realized something else. I'd rather worry about you up close than from afar."

"I like the sound of that." His lips caught hers, and she melted in a puddle at his feet.

When he pulled away, she followed, offering her lips again.

"There's something else."

"Enough with the talk," she said as he dodged her.

He knelt in front of her and her breath caught. "Will you marry me?"

"Ahem." She turned and saw Natalie standing in front of the chapel with friends, family and onlookers. "If you'll say yes, maybe we can get on with this wedding. Y'all are kind of stealing Trent and Faith's thunder."

Caitlyn giggled and turned back to Mitch. "Yes."

Applause and whistles echoed through the air.

Ten wasted years. But they wouldn't waste any more of the precious time God had allotted them.

"I always wanted my own personal rodeo queen." Mitch stood and pulled her into his arms.

"I always wanted my own personal Texas Ranger."

He claimed her lips, and his kiss told the tale—the yearning of ten years apart and the lifetime ahead of them.

\* \* \* \* \*

# REQUEST YOUR FREE BOOKS!

## 2 FREE CHRISTIAN NOVELS
## PLUS 2
# FREE
## MYSTERY GIFTS

HEARTSONG
PRESENTS

---

**YES!** Please send me 2 Free Heartsong Presents novels and my 2 FREE mystery gifts (gifts are worth about $10). After receiving them, if I don't wish to receive any more books I can return the shipping statement marked "cancel." If I don't cancel, I will receive 4 brand-new novels every month and be billed just $4.24 per book in the U.S. and $5.24 per book in Canada. That's a savings of at least 20% off the cover price. It's quite a bargain! Shipping and handling is just 50¢ per book in the U.S. and 75¢ per book in Canada.* I understand that accepting the 2 free books and gifts places me under no obligation to buy anything. I can always return a shipment and cancel at any time. Even if I never buy another book, the two free books and gifts are mine to keep forever.

159/359 HDN FVYK

| | | |
|---|---|---|
| Name | (PLEASE PRINT) | |
| Address | | Apt. # |
| City | State | Zip |

Signature (if under 18, a parent or guardian must sign)

### Mail to the **Harlequin®** Reader Service:
### IN U.S.A.: P.O. Box 1867, Buffalo, NY 14240-1867

* Terms and prices subject to change without notice. Prices do not include applicable taxes. Sales tax applicable in N.Y. This offer is limited to one order per household. Not valid for current subscribers to Heartsong Presents books. All orders subject to credit approval. Credit or debit balances in a customer's account(s) may be offset by any other outstanding balance owed by or to the customer. Please allow 4 to 6 weeks for delivery. Offer available while quantities last. Offer valid only in the U.S.

**Your Privacy**—The Harlequin® Reader Service is committed to protecting your privacy. Our Privacy Policy is available online at www.ReaderService.com or upon request from the Harlequin Reader Service.
We make a portion of our mailing list available to reputable third parties that offer products we believe may interest you. If you prefer that we not exchange your name with third parties, or if you wish to clarify or modify your communication preferences, please visit us at www.ReaderService.com/consumerchoice or write to us at Harlequin Reader Service Preference Service, P.O. Box 9062, Buffalo, NY 14269. Include your complete name and address.

HSPDIR13R

# REQUEST YOUR FREE BOOKS!

## 2 FREE INSPIRATIONAL NOVELS
## PLUS 2
## FREE
## MYSTERY GIFTS

*Love Inspired*
# HISTORICAL
### INSPIRATIONAL HISTORICAL ROMANCE

---

**YES!** Please send me 2 FREE Love Inspired® Historical novels and my 2 FREE mystery gifts (gifts are worth about $10). After receiving them, if I don't wish to receive any more books, I can return the shipping statement marked "cancel." If I don't cancel, I will receive 4 brand-new novels every month and be billed just $4.74 per book in the U.S. or $5.24 per book in Canada. That's a savings of at least 21% off the cover price. It's quite a bargain! Shipping and handling is just 50¢ per book in the U.S. and 75¢ per book in Canada.* I understand that accepting the 2 free books and gifts places me under no obligation to buy anything. I can always return a shipment and cancel at any time. Even if I never buy another book, the two free books and gifts are mine to keep forever.

102/302 IDN F5CY

| | |
|---|---|
| Name | (PLEASE PRINT) |
| Address | Apt. # |
| City | State/Prov. | Zip/Postal Code |

Signature (if under 18, a parent or guardian must sign)

### Mail to the Harlequin® Reader Service:
**IN U.S.A.:** P.O. Box 1867, Buffalo, NY 14240-1867
**IN CANADA:** P.O. Box 609, Fort Erie, Ontario L2A 5X3

**Want to try two free books from another series?**
**Call 1-800-873-8635 or visit www.ReaderService.com.**

\* Terms and prices subject to change without notice. Prices do not include applicable taxes. Sales tax applicable in N.Y. Canadian residents will be charged applicable taxes. Offer not valid in Quebec. This offer is limited to one order per household. Not valid for current subscribers to Love Inspired Historical books. All orders subject to credit approval. Credit or debit balances in a customer's account(s) may be offset by any other outstanding balance owed by or to the customer. Please allow 4 to 6 weeks for delivery. Offer available while quantities last.

**Your Privacy**—The Harlequin® Reader Service is committed to protecting your privacy. Our Privacy Policy is available online at www.ReaderService.com or upon request from the Harlequin Reader Service.

We make a portion of our mailing list available to reputable third parties that offer products we believe may interest you. If you prefer that we not exchange your name with third parties, or if you wish to clarify or modify your communication preferences, please visit us at www.ReaderService.com/consumerschoice or write to us at Harlequin Reader Service Preference Service, P.O. Box 9062, Buffalo, NY 14269. Include your complete name and address.

LIHDIR13R

# REQUEST YOUR FREE BOOKS!

## 2 FREE INSPIRATIONAL NOVELS
## PLUS 2
## FREE
## MYSTERY GIFTS

*Love Inspired*

**YES!** Please send me 2 FREE Love Inspired® novels and my 2 FREE mystery gifts (gifts are worth about $10). After receiving them, if I don't wish to receive any more books, I can return the shipping statement marked "cancel." If I don't cancel, I will receive 6 brand-new novels every month and be billed just $4.74 per book in the U.S. or $5.24 per book in Canada. That's a savings of at least 21% off the cover price. It's quite a bargain! Shipping and handling is just 50¢ per book in the U.S. and 75¢ per book in Canada.* I understand that accepting the 2 free books and gifts places me under no obligation to buy anything. I can always return a shipment and cancel at any time. Even if I never buy another book, the two free books and gifts are mine to keep forever.

105/305 IDN F49N

| Name | | |
|------|------|------|
| | (PLEASE PRINT) | |

| Address | | Apt. # |
|---------|------|--------|

| City | State/Prov. | Zip/Postal Code |
|------|-------------|-----------------|

Signature (if under 18, a parent or guardian must sign)

### Mail to the **Harlequin® Reader Service:**
**IN U.S.A.:** P.O. Box 1867, Buffalo, NY 14240-1867
**IN CANADA:** P.O. Box 609, Fort Erie, Ontario L2A 5X3

**Are you a subscriber to Love Inspired books
and want to receive the larger-print edition?
Call 1-800-873-8635 or visit www.ReaderService.com.**